Fit to be tied

His cell mate ran over and grabbed Slocum by the shoulders. "You've got to stop them. You can't let them hang me."

"Not much I can do. No gun, nothing."

"You can't let them." Then Howie backed slow-like away from him, looking down in disbelief at his crotch, where he had pissed all over himself. He turned, shaking the bars again, and began to scream, "Sheriff Watson! Save me!"

The mob swarmed the office and then burst into the jail, unlocked the door, and took the hysterical Howie by the arms. Then they stopped and the four of them looked for a split second at Slocum.

"What's *he* in here for?" they asked.

"Some bounty hunters made a big mistake," Slocum began to plead. "A telegram coming tomorrow will clear me."

"Hang him too," someone shouted and dragged him out of the cell after Howie.

Slocum's hands were soon bound tightly with a rope behind his back. It bit into his already-sore wrists. He was thrown into the dark street by two men. Someone pulled a flour-sack hood down over his head and he could see no more. The two men steered Slocum to the gallows.

Chants of "string 'em up" roared in Slocum's ears . . .

DON'T MISS THESE
ALL-ACTION WESTERN SERIES
FROM THE BERKLEY PUBLISHING GROUP

THE GUNSMITH by J. R. Roberts
> Clint Adams was a legend among lawmen, outlaws and ladies. They called him . . . the Gunsmith.

LONGARM by Tabor Evans
> The popular long-running series about Deputy U.S. Marshal Long—his life, his loves, his fight for justice.

SLOCUM by Jake Logan
> Today's longest-running action Western. John Slocum rides a deadly trail of hot blood and cold steel.

BUSHWHACKERS by B. J. Lanagan
> An action-packed series by the creators of *Longarm*! The rousing adventures of the most brutal gang of cutthroats ever assembled—Quantrill's Raiders.

DIAMONDBACK by Guy Brewer
> Dex Yancey is Diamondback, a Southern gentleman turned con man when his brother cheats him out of the family fortune. Ladies love him. Gamblers hate him. But nobody pulls one over on Dex. . . .

WILDGUN by Jack Hanson
> The blazing adventures of mountain man Will Barlow—from the creators of *Longarm*!

TEXAS TRACKER by Tom Calhoun
> Meet J. T. Law: the most relentless and dangerous manhunter in all Texas. Where sheriffs and posses fail, he's the best man to bring in the most vicious outlaws—for a price.

JAKE LOGAN

SLOCUM'S DISGUISE

JOVE BOOKS, NEW YORK

This is a work of fiction. Names, characters, places, and incidents either are the product of the author's imagination or are used fictitiously, and any resemblance to actual persons, living or dead, business establishments, events, or locales is entirely coincidental.

SLOCUM'S DISGUISE

A Jove Book / published by arrangement with
the author

PRINTING HISTORY
Jove edition / November 2002

Visit our website at
www.penguinputnam.com

ISBN: 0-515-13405-8

A JOVE BOOK®
Jove Books are published by The Berkley Publishing Group,
a division of Penguin Putnam Inc.,
375 Hudson Street, New York, New York 10014.
JOVE and the "J" design
are trademarks belonging to Penguin Putnam Inc.

PRINTED IN THE UNITED STATES OF AMERICA

10 9 8 7 6 5 4 3 2 1

1

"Make one damned move and you're dead meat," someone growled in his ear. A voice so close he knew he wasn't dreaming, as he fought to awaken from a hard sleep. The blanket over him was jerked away. A cold chill swept over the bare skin on his upper torso, not so much from the room's temperature, but from the fear that gathered inside his numb brain about the seriousness of the situation at hand.

Someone dragged Rosa kicking and thrashing out of the bed from beside him. Her screams shattered the early morning quiet. Slocum looked over in time to see her abductor jerk her head back with a fist full of her hair. Then in a flash of his knife blade, he slit her throat. Blood sprayed all over her white shift, and to reinforce his order the second intruder shoved the gunpowder-smelling muzzle of his Colt into Slocum's face. Rosa's last gurgling sounds ground deep into Slocum's soul and forced back a bitter sourness behind his tongue.

The metallic sound of the pistol's hammer being locked back in a click brought him back to the stark reality of the moment. In the depths of his sleep-fogged mind, he promised that her death would not go unavenged. Nothing he could do for her now, but these heartless butchers would pay for this, if he managed to live that long.

Trying hard to make out both of the killers in the yellow-red dawn light that speared into the room, he noticed the fancy beaded holster tie-downs strapped on the killer's leg. He rose slowly and studied the man who wiped the blade of his Green River knife on her shift. Full-faced, the killer looked like a squat toad—short built and fat, with cold fish eyes. What did he expect from a savage who'd so senselessly murdered a sweet dove like Rosa and showed the same scorn for her still body he'd have showed a dead dog.

"Well, Slocum, how you going to like swinging from a rope in Fort Scott." His bugged out eyes met Slocum's gaze in the dim light. Then he laughed and smirked like a man filled with confidence. "Me and Del been tracking you ever since you left Kanab, Utah."

"The warrant's run out," Slocum said and reached for his pants.

"Good try. But we've got a new one being wired to us. Along with five hundred dollars reward in American coin," the bounty hunter shouted, with his head thrown back in manic excitement.

Dumbstruck, Slocum pulled on his britches and sat on the edge of the bed. The killer walked over and planted his dusty knee-high boot on the mattress beside him. While Slocum didn't trust the two, he wanted to be completely dressed before they dragged him out of the hovel. No need for him to be naked, in jail or wherever they took him. He'd sure need all his clothes if the opportunity came where he could escape these two madmen. Ignoring them, he reached for his boot.

"I didn't hear your name," he said.

"Radamacher's mine. That's Del, short for Delaware."

"Guess our paths have never crossed before," Slocum said and started to put on his boot. He'd never heard of either of them, but bounty hunters were a nickel a dozen in the West.

"Hold it!" Del ordered. With his whisker-bristled face, he was the taller of the two. He jerked the boot from Slocum's grasp, reached inside and produced the small .30-caliber revolver that Slocum kept concealed in the vamp.

"You won't need this where you're going." Del grinned, wagging the pistol in Slocum's face. Then he stuck it in his belt.

"Good," Radamacher said in appreciation to his partner.

One trick lost. Slocum took the boot back and shoved his toe in it. He felt grateful he didn't have to stare at the dead little whore and the bloody mess on the other side of the bed as he dressed. Why kill her? So she couldn't get him help to escape? No telling how bounty men's minds worked. Lucky to be alive, but the old warrants said the reward was to be paid for his capture alive. He'd already be in Hades with poor Rosa if it had been printed dead or alive. In those cases, bounty hunters brought the outlaw's head back in a tow sack. They didn't have to feed their captive that way, and he couldn't escape, unless a hole came in the bag.

"How did you guys find me?" Slocum asked, waiting for Radamacher to finish inspecting and then to hand him the second boot.

"It wasn't hard. You left a good track coming down here from Wyoming."

Slocum wondered about ranchers along the trail out of Colorado and those folks that fed men on the run, no questions asked. Had this pair killed any of them? They might have acted like men hiding out and used that to gain the confidence of the way stations down through the four corners country and eventually to the border and Sonora. He didn't want to think about what these two bloodthirsty killers might have done on his back trail.

He indicated his shirt on the chair, then waited for Radamacher to pick it up and feel for anything in it before he tossed it at him. Slocum slid his arm in the sleeve and buttoned it up.

"Where you taking me?"

"Lordsburg."

Slocum closed one eye and looked pained at Radamacher. "Why up there?"

"Ha, we know you've got lots of friends all along this border. Up there, you'll be rotting in jail when them two Kansas deputies can get there on the Southern Pacific."

"Them deputies?"

"Yeah, the Abbott brothers. You must know them by now. Put your hands out."

Radamacher snapped the hand shackles on his wrists. "Get up. You try anything, you can lay in that Lordburg's jail—wounded."

"You hear him, tough guy?" Del asked.

"Nothing's wrong with my ears."

"Get your saddle," Radamacher said and shoved Slocum toward it when he stood up.

With his manacled hands, he picked the saddle up by the horn but was unable to get the blankets. Radamacher threw the pads over his shoulders. The smell of sour horse sweat from his saddle blankets filled his nose as he headed for the doorway.

Outside, three horses stood by the corral. Rose's small cur dog lay dead in the dust, obviously killed to silence his barking. In the east, the full ball of dawn had come over the saw-edged mountains. Gambrel quail whistled out in the chaparral. It was a two-day ride to Lordsburg, and somewhere on that route Slocum needed to outsmart this pair and escape.

Radamacher saddled the bay for him, complaining as he pulled on the cinch. "This old sumbitch ain't worth much." He strained to tighten the girth. "All told I figure that your horse, gear and guns ain't going to bring us more than thirty bucks. Kinda living on the poor side, ain't yeah?"

Slocum shook his head. Up until these two arrived, he had slept regularly with the woman they killed. Rosa had plenty of cabrito, brown beans, red wine to wash the tender goat meat down with and some mescal to drink at night. Up until those two burst in, he thought, he was living pretty rich.

"Ha, we captured the big outlaw and he's poor as a damn Messikin," Radamacher said, jerking down the right stirrup and turning to indicate for him to mount up. When Slocum reached with both hands for the saddle horn, Del rode in and took the reins.

A guarded pair, Slocum noted—what one of them didn't think about, the other did. It would not be any easy deal to outfox them, but if they ever let up, he'd try to be ready to make good his escape. In the saddle, he clasped the horn in his chained hands and they left Rosa's place in a long trot. Several Spanish nannies ran bleating into the mesquite brush, their small bells ringing as they escaped the riders who headed north, ignoring them.

Slocum could soon see the outlines of the Muleshoes and the Swisshelms Mountains on the left as they crossed the open country of the San Pedro drainage. A broad valley between the two ranges was carpeted with sun-cured brown grass. Wagon ruts bisected it that linked trade with northern Mexico and the new steel rails of the Southern Pacific inching westward into the Arizona Territory. Mining activity in that area of southeast Arizona Territory was also picking up, while the booming silver helldorado of Tombstone lay fifty miles west-by-north beyond the Muleshoe Mountains. To the right were the hills that resembled cakes of brown sugar, thus their name, Pentacillos.

A clear azure sky was overhead, and a few yellow meadowlarks whistled at their passing. With Del in the lead, holding his reins and Radamacher behind with a scattergun over his lap and ready—Slocum settled in for the long ride. These two were tough, and he knew it would require a miracle for him to ever get away from them. Still, inside the Lordsburg jail his chances to escape might even be less.

Bareheaded, he regretted not getting his hat back there; a day or so in the sun would blister his untanned forehead. Too many things to think about. Besides, he was still sick in his heart over Rosa's cruel demise; they would pay for that someday. He swore that would happen.

Pushing the horses hard, Slocum noted how both men kept looking a lot over their shoulders, acting anxious, as if they expected pursuit. He couldn't figure who that would be. Perhaps some relatives of hers would look for them to avenge her murder, but he knew of no organized posse that would see about some Mexican *puta*'s welfare.

Good—if the two were on edge over the threat of someone coming to his rescue, he might use that to his own advantage. One thing for certain, the small bay horse he rode couldn't outrun their horses in a race to the dark junipers that clad the lower foothills. He judged the distance five miles away to the fringe of the grass. Damn, he'd been in hard places like this before and things worked out; he simply needed to keep his eyes and mind open for that opportunity to escape.

Somewhere, a couple of ravens cawed noisily at them. Both men forced their animals to keep up the grinding trot. Midday, Slocum could have drank a horse trough full of water, and his empty belly complained at his backbone. No letup as the towering peaks of the Chiricahuas drew closer; ahead the shiny playas, like inland seas, began to shimmer in the high sun bearing down on them.

The creak of saddle leather, drum of hooves and the lathered horses' hard breathing were the sounds that filled his mind when in late afternoon they finally were forced to walk their weary animals and headed east into the hills that they must cross to reach Lordsburg.

Somewhere in this area of sagebrush and sun-fired grass was the New Mexico–Arizona Territory line; Slocum knew it bisected this country north to south. Perhaps the bounty hunters felt less threat in the jurisdiction of Santa Fe than they did in Arizona. Neither man said much, besides grumbling at their horses for not moving faster.

Slocum could see the two acted more at ease the closer they got to New Mexico. Perhaps they figured they'd out-ridden any pursuit. Whatever the reason, the bounty hunters became relaxed when they finally rode the eastbound main road that paralleled the shiny new ribbons of steel on the fresh-cut wooden ties. The dirt-work fills in the grade were still unsettled looking too. Slocum had no interest in this transportation system; his mind was still keen on escaping, despite the blistering sun on his face.

At their current rate of travel, they'd deliver him to Lordsburg's sheriff before midnight, if they didn't cripple one of the horses. Too dry to draw spittle, his tongue felt swollen enough to fill his mouth. They were a tough pair, for they'd had no water either since before dawn, if then, and carried none on their saddles. Not once did they make any effort to find any either, though most sources would have been aside in the fringes of the San Pedro Valley, in places like Turkey Creek and Skeleton Canyon.

They pushed eastward as the sun dropped lower in the west. Lots of yucca and century plants dotted the land. Not much traffic on the road, save some outfit camped beside the way with their skinny teams unhooked from their overstuffed, rickety wagons. The bony stock looked up from their grazing as the three rode past their roadside positions for the night. Smoke from her cooking fire swirled around a woman's waist as she straightened and wiped her sweaty face on her sleeve. Tall, lean as a willow, Slocum saw her green eyes glint like precious cut stones. Strange her head was without the sunbonnet that most of her peers wore against the sun's erosive effects on their facial skin.

They must be going to the promised land of milk and honey. Just over the next ridge, Slocum bet her husband had told her when they left the last place. Nothing ahead of her but more hell, cactus, dry camps and the acrid dirt on her teeth for a thousand miles if they survived it. In the south, a twisting dust devil danced across the land of sun-cured grass and greasewood brush. Something else to taunt her ability to mentally survive in this hell should it swirl through her camp.

Soon his thoughts about the woman were lost in the dirt road boiling up to clog his nose and eyes. The heat of the sun all day without a hat had taken a toll on his own awareness. Where were the Abbott brothers? Coming to get him, they said. But from where? How much time did he have before the pair of Kansas deputies arrived?

His wrists were raw from the handcuffs chaffing them. Besides the ache in his chest, the sharp knife of hunger and thirst sapped his strength. Despite his efforts to rise above the waves of weariness that swarmed his thinking, he knew he couldn't muster much more effort than to hang on and ride as their prisoner.

How much longer could those two hang on? The miles had taken a toll on them too. The long shadows before them, he didn't need to look back and know the sun was setting behind them. Somewhere behind the Chiricahuas and Dos Cabezos, the sun would sink from sight. Be an hour of twilight, then only the stars to guide them. There should be starlight enough for a man to ride this road. *Whew.* He tried to shake his exhaustion, the sadness of Rosa's death that further depressed him and the radiant heat's efforts to bake his head into an earthen pot.

At last, in the night, he could make out the twinkling

lights of Lordsburg. The road slanted downhill and the scattered flickers were still ten miles away.

"Get your damn horse moving," Radamacher said to Del and whipped Slocum's bay with his reins. He might have saved his effort slashing the tired pony, but the smaller horse finally began to trot as he persisted to repeatedly beat him.

An hour later, they drew up at a rock-adobe building. A lamp on the porch shone on the barred windows. The hoosegow, Slocum figured. A tall, lean figure with a badge on his vest came out and looked them over.

"Howdy," Radamacher said and dropped out of the saddle. He tried to find his sea legs and at last rested with his arms thrown over the hitch rail. "We've got that bastard, Slocum."

"Hmm," the lawman said, and turned his head sideways to look at Slocum. "About done them horses in, didn't ya?"

"With that reward, I can buy more."

"Been a-thinking about that. You'll owe me for keeping him till that Kansas law gets here."

"How much?" Radamacher demanded.

"Two bucks a day."

"Hell, they won't be long—"

"I figure about fifty days," the law said and folded his arms over his chest.

"Fifty days? Hell, they could come from China in that time."

"You don't understand. I'm the one's got to verify this is really who you say he is. See, you might have hired this hombre to play the part. Can't take no chances and pay the wrong reward to the wrong parties, right?"

"It's him, all right."

"What's your name?" the sheriff asked, looking up at Slocum.

"Jeb Dun. Tried to tell them that this morning."

"He's lying," Radamacher shouted.

"This sumbitch's John Slocum," Del said, booting his horse in closer.

"How can I be certain he ain't who he says he is?" the sheriff asked, working his shakedown scheme upon the two bounty men.

Despite his discomfort, Slocum wanted to laugh out loud at the predicament those two were in. They'd be lucky to collect more than half that total reward money; this lawman was no dummy. He probably made fifty a month as salary and the rest came as small kickbacks each week from the various saloons and whorehouses around town. Here was a prime chance to sweeten his bankroll. The bounty hunters needed him, much more than he needed them. They had no standing in the community; who could they press charges against? What were the facts of the case? No, Radamacher and Delaware would have to accept what he wanted them to have of the reward monies.

"Bring Dun inside," the lawman said, then he turned on his heel and went through the lighted doorway.

"His goddamn name ain't Dun," Radamacher grumbled after the lawman. "His name's Slocum."

The pair roughly jerked Slocum down, and once on his feet, he shrugged away their hands. Headed for the doorway, he wasn't about to take any more from the pair.

"Give me the key to them cuffs," the lawman said. "Well, Dun or Slocum, whoever the hell you are, my name's Troy Watson. You get any funny ideas about a jailbreak before we clear this up about your identity, you better have a casket picked out."

"Is there a lawyer in this burg?" Slocum asked, holding his hands out to be freed from the chaffing cuffs at last.

"Yeah, but not until in the morning. Meanwhile, I'm wiring Fort Scott and asking for a list of scars and birthmarks that this Slocum has. You ain't the man that they say you are, a night in this jail won't kill you."

"I damn sure am not this Slocum fellow that they claim I am."

"We'll sort that out tomorrow. Here." He tossed the cuffs to Radamacher. Then he shoved Slocum toward the cell block with a set of keys in his other hand from the hook on the wall.

"You got any food or water? They never gave me none all day," Slocum said, glaring back at the front door, where the two bounty hunters stood, busy talking to each other in low tones. Obviously they were pissed by Watson's shakedown, but not much of anything they could do about it—the only satisfaction Slocum got out of the entire day.

"You can have a bucket of water. Can't get any food till sunup. Café's already closed."

In the cell, Slocum sipped water from a gourd that Watson provided. He didn't need the belly cramps from drinking too much water too fast. To cool off some more, he poured some over his feverish head. In the outer office he could hear them arguing, Watson and the pair. Those bounty hunters might as well have saved their breath; this time Watson held the upper hand.

After recovering some, Slocum spread the sweat-smelling blanket on the iron cot. He decided to try and sleep. The rest might restore some of his thinking. When Watson got the Kansas reply, he might decide he was not Jeb Dun. It was worth the chance to try anything.

Slocum awoke with a start. A struggle in the outer office and lots of loud angry voices caused him to bolt upright. For a second, he thought he was back at the earlier scene and he wanted to shout, *No, Rosa*, to save her. Instead, two men wrestled with a prisoner between them. Another man unlocked the cell and they hurled him inside. The barred door shut with a clang.

"There, you rapist bastard!" one of the out-of-breath men shouted.

"Should've cut his balls out," another said, tucking in his shirttail and looking hard at the new prisoner in the half-light that filtered in from the outer room.

"I never done nothing!" the prisoner screamed, pressing himself against the bars. "I swear to God, I never touched her."

"You son of a bitch—" The other two had to drag the red-faced man back to prevent him from assaulting the prisoner through the bars.

"Who the hell are you?" the prisoner asked, blinking at Slocum, then turning back and slumping against the iron bars.

"Jeb Dun. An innocent man here by mistaken identity."

"Me too," the thin man said.

Slocum guessed him to be in his late teens. They had called him a rapist; obviously they were upset over the matter. After they left the cell area, the threesome spoke about going and finding the sheriff.

"They say you raped someone?" Slocum asked, rubbing the back of his neck and trying to wake up.

"They don't understand. She wasn't no virgin."

"Oh—"

"Yeah, I seen Joey Weams screwing her on the back porch. But she was too good to let me have any—that bitch!"

"Too good, huh?"

"Yeah, the little bitch."

"Guess you fixed her?"

"Yeah, I did." He began to laugh, first slow-like then louder and louder. "I tied her hands and gagged her so she couldn't scream. Then I put her belly down over a barrel. You ever do it like that? Put a slut like her over a barrel, throw up her dress and stick it to her?" He repeatedly hunched his crotch out as if demonstrating how he did it.

"They catch you doing it?"

"Yeah, but not before I got her three times." He showed the count with his spread out fingers.

"Whew. Three times?" Slocum shook his head as if impressed.

"Yeah, three times—I guess the gag I stuck in her mouth must have finally choked her, cause she never squirmed the last time when I stuck my pecker in her. I still did it anyway." He shook his head disappointedly. "Wasn't as good either."

Slocum shuddered at the thought of the heinous crime. "How old was she?"

"Why, old enough to bleed, old enough to butcher," he said with his chest stuck out.

"How old?"

"She'd be twelve soon." And he sneered at Slocum as if that was plenty old enough for him.

Slocum shook his head and wanted to vomit. First, a perfectly good woman was murdered, partially his fault, and now an innocent child was dead at the hands of another maniac. The whole damn world was coming apart at the seams.

"My name's Howie."

"Dun."

"Guess we're in here for a while. What did you do?"

"Nothing, they arrested the wrong person. Bounty hunters made a mistake."

"Really? Jesus, that's bad."

"You're telling me." He turned an ear and listened. In front of the jail, a crowd was gathering. Plenty of loud, angry voices were demanding justice. That only meant one thing: vigilantes. Howie's crime had exceeded the moral standards of the community. Sometimes a simple horse theft triggered it, but once their fuse was lit—nothing could stop them. People on the frontier had little patience with slow-moving courts and what they meted out as justice. A rope, and perhaps even a sharp knife first, might suit them in this case.

"What're they doing out there?' Howie asked, his eyes big as saucers. He clung to the cell bars and tried to see into the outer office.

"They're working up their nerve to bust in here and sentence us."

"Sentence us?" he asked in a high-pitched voice.

"Yeah, you better go to praying and make your own deal with your maker."

"Deal with my maker?" He ran over and grabbed Slocum by the shoulders. "You've got to stop them. You can't let them hang me."

"Not much I can do. No gun, nothing—"

"You can't let them—" Then Howie backed slow-like away for him, looking down in disbelief at his own darkening crotch where he had pissed all over himself. He turned, shaking the bars again, and began to scream, "Sheriff Watson! Save me!"

The mob swarmed the office and then the jail. The rattle of keys was punctuated with their sharp words: "Hang the sumbitch." "Cut him first. I've got a knife." "Yeah, do that." "Stick it in his ass." "Yeah, I'd like for him to scream like that little girl must have."

They burst into the jail portion, unlocked the door with a look of determination written on their faces and took the hysterical Howie by the arms. Then they stopped and the four of them looked for a split second at Slocum.

"What's he in here for?" They searched each other's face for the answer.

"Probably horse stealing," someone said.

"No! Hey, some bounty hunters made a big mistake," he managed to plead. "The telegram in the morning will clear me."

"Hang him too," someone shouted and in a flash took Slocum by the arms and dragged him out of the cell after the whining Howie.

Slocum's hands were soon bound tightly in a rope behind his back. It bit into his already sore wrists. He was propelled into the dark street by a man on each side. Lamps and lanterns were being held up by the crowd. Someone pulled a flour-sack hood down over his head and he could see no more. The main attention of the mob centered on the blubbering Howie, but a man on each arm steered Slocum down the dirt street to their eventual gallows.

The chants of "string 'em up" roared in Slocum's ears.

"We're saving New Mexico lots of money," the guy on his left said.

"Yeah," his partner said on the other side. "Sumbitch like this one gets out of prison, he'd just steal another horse."

"Never stole no horse—" Slocum tried to protest.

"Yeah, we know you're innocent. Here, get on this horse." They physically loaded him into the saddle. Slocum could see nothing for the mask. His toes at last found the stirrup.

"Get them ropes over that limb," a voice of authority shouted.

In his world of blindness, Slocum tried hard to even breathe as he sat on the flighty horse. He could feel how the crowd's noise and the excitement made the animal he sat on perilously restless. Shifting around, the pony knocked into people who cursed him and slapped him with the flat of their hands. Any minute Slocum expected to feel a noose being placed around his neck.

He could hear Howie screaming—pleading for his life. The angry remarks of the lynch mob sounded all around Slocum; the horse danced underneath him despite the efforts of the man holding the reins to control him. The

final seconds of Slocum's life flashed before him; he was
going out of the world over a mistake. How bad could
one day turn out to be? Less than twenty-four hours ago
the pair had awakened him and savagely killed poor Rosa;
now he would be lynched.

Shame too—because neither them two nor the greedy
sheriff would ever collect that reward for him *alive*.

"Whoa!" the horse holder shouted as the pony shied
from something.

In an instant, Slocum realized the spooked horse had
jerked the reins loose from the holder. At the top of his
lungs, Slocum screamed like a banshee from behind the
flour sack and jammed both heels in the animal's side.
The immediate bolt came within inches of unseating him.
Hands tied behind him, he had no way to guide the pony,
nor could he see a thing for the flour sack over his head.
All he could do was pound him with his boot heels and
shout from under the cotton bag.

The horse must have breasted aside a couple vigilantes
in his charge, for Slocum felt the bumps, then in a full-
out run, he leaned forward and the pony flat raced. Bullets
whizzed past like hornets, but they only sped the horse,
and the angry shouts of the mob grew farther and farther
behind.

Slocum and the crazed horse flew away into a world
of darkness; he was unable to see or to control him. But
soon there was only the sound of hard breathing, pound-
ing hooves, saddle leather squeaking in protest and the
gurgle of the horse's stomach as he stretched out harder
to escape the fears behind him.

After the pony carried him over some steep grades, he
slowed to a lope. Something in the night spooked him,
perhaps a flushed owl, and he tore away again. Slocum
felt certain the horse must be on the road headed west.
He recalled how at first the horse had swung around and
run back down the street in the direction they came from.

But where the crazed animal was headed besides that he had little idea. Perhaps to a ranch or the place where he came from—no telling.

How would he ever get the sack off his head? His hands remained tied despite the herculean efforts that only made the hemp cut deeper into the skin around his wrists. All he could do was ride, and pray the horse's heart did not give out before he was beyond the grasp of the mob. *Lord help me.*

2

"Who're you?"

Slocum opened his eyes and looked up in disbelief. The sack off his head, the bright sun hurt his eyes to stare at the menacing shape brandishing some kind of club. How long had he been out? No telling; it was morning. He lay in some brittle dry bunchgrass with the smell of creosote from the greasewood filling his nose.

It was a woman. Hatless. Was it the same one he'd seen the day before at the wagon? The honyocker bunch on the road?

"Slocum," he managed. "Untie me."

"How did you get here?" she asked with the sound of caution in her voice.

"Long story," he managed in a hoarse voice that shocked even him.

He rolled over to show her his bound hands. The stiff grass stems poked him in the face—no matter, he needed to be loose.

"Who did this?" she asked.

When he glanced back, he felt better. She had knelt down to do something. Where was the horse? He tried to look around as he felt her fingers fumble with the knots.

18

"You're bleeding," she said.

"Not surprised," he said. Both of his wrists felt on fire from the actions of the rope and his long struggle to get free of it.

"I can't get them loose. They'll have to be cut."

"You got a knife?"

"Not with me. I was out looking for wood. Tired of burning them cow chips."

"Don't blame you." He managed, still tied, to roll back over.

"How did you get like this anyway?"

"Couple of bounty hunters took me to jail, thought I was Jeb Dun. Then a mob broke in the jail to hang some lowlife and they drug me out with him." He felt her hand steady his shoulder as he came to his knees. Light-headed, things swarmed around him. No sign of the horse across the endless flat desert that stretched to some hazy, distant, sawtooth mountains, which probably were down in Mexico. His mount must have run on, whenever he stumbled and unceremoniously dumped Slocum on the ground—he tried to think when that had been. During the night was all he could recall.

"You going to make it?' she asked, sounding concerned.

"Sure," he said and rocked on unsteady legs with his hands still tied. He did not feel very handy even at standing. Whew, he was weak.

"It's a ways to the wagon."

"I'll make it. What's your name?"

"Cyra Glasscow."

"Miss or Mrs?"

"Mrs. My man died six months ago. I'm traveling with my brother-in-law and another man."

"Oh."

"They're both widowers too."

"Where you headed?"

"Tombstone, if we can get there."

"Having trouble?"

"Yes, this morning they took a wheel back to Lords-burg to get a rim shrunk. Couldn't keep it on the wheel. I told them to have it done when we were through there. They thought they'd find water to soak the wheel in and swell the wood, but, of course, there isn't any out here."

She rubbed her eyebrow with a finger as if considering him, and he noticed the rich brown tan on her face. High cheekbones, with a nose perhaps too large; her small mouth made "ohs" when she spoke, and her green eyes, he recalled from the day before, were the color of waving velvet Kansas wheat.

The wash-faded denim dress she wore was closed at the throat and then went down in a row of matching buttons over her small bustline to a slender waist, before it flared out to give her legs freedom. Toes of her moccasins peeked out from under the hem.

He guessed her to be in her mid-twenties despite the premature gray strands in her brown hair that was up in a bun at the back of her head. Ready to head for the wagon, he nodded for her to go first. Still wondering about the horse and where it went, he set out to follow her. Her arms full of the precious sticks, she led the way.

"How did they make such a mistake? I mean thinking you were this Jeb Dun?"

"Bounty hunters are a greedy lot. No scruples. They'd try anything to collect a reward."

"This mob?"

"They broke in the jail to hang a man who had as-saulted a small girl."

"And why take you?"

"Mob's don't have any brains. They come to hang someone, they hang whoever's there." When his toe caught on something, he was forced to run forward to keep upright.

"You okay?" she asked with a frown of concern and squinting against the sun.

"Ain't very handy having your hands tied."

"I'd say not, but I could not get the rope undone."

"It's fine, Cyra. I'll be okay." He paused and regained his breath. Across the desert ahead, in the shimmering heat waves, he could see the faded yellow canvas tops of their two wagons.

"You married?"

"No, ma'am."

She looked back to be certain he was coming after her. "A mule kicked Rand in the head. He never recovered."

"Sorry."

"No one could help it. You marry a man and start down a road you figure will be your whole life, then you come to the spot where the road ends and you wander aimlessly from there on."

"You wandering?"

"Yes, I would say that." She threw back her head as if to free herself of something. "I agreed to come west with them to find myself a new road."

"You like them?"

"They're good men. Would I marry them? No." She started the descent into the dry creek bed.

After her, Slocum found his footing down the steep cow trail that led to the bottom of the wash. She waited with her arms full of the wood at the bottom and watched to be sure he could make it.

"Why not marry one of them?"

"They're both dreamers. They plan to go to Tombstone and get rich."

"What's wrong with that?"

"How many ever hit the big strike? I mean, how many of the hundreds and thousands of men swarming to these mother-lode towns ever get rich?"

"Not many, but some get comfortable."

"You looking to get rich?"

"No, I'm looking to get by."

She nodded as if satisfied, turned, and they started up the far side—her going first. He thought once he'd be forced to fall on his knees to save his balance, but he made the top and drew a deep breath. Nodding to her that he was fine, he followed her on.

At the wagon, she cut his binds and went after something to doctor his cuts.

Grateful to have his limbs free at last, he flung them around like windmills to get the stiffness out. She returned with some creamy salve in a jar. "Rub that on those raw places. It'll heal quicker."

On her toes, she made a look of disapproval at his forehead. "Put some up there too. You're blistered. I've got an old straw hat if you'd like it."

"Sure," he said, winching at the pain in his wrists as he rubbed in the soothing cream.

His head treated with her salve, he nodded to her gift of the filthy, near-rotten straw sombrero. Still, it would protect his head from the rising sun and heat.

"Now you look like a Mexican."

"Good," he said, hoping the disguise would work.

"Horses are coming," she said. Her look cut around and questioned him.

He heard them by then and shrugged.

"Get under the wagon and act asleep. I'll handle them."

"I can't hide behind your skirts—"

"No time to argue, get under the wagon. We don't have time to talk about this."

The dust from their horses came into sight. Nothing to do but obey her. If he only had a weapon, a pistol or anything. Underneath the wagon box, he pulled the blanket over himself and used the sombrero to cover his head.

He could hear them rein up their hard breathing horses.

"Ma'am. We're looking for a horse thief that stole a fancy racehorse last night."

"I saw no racehorse."

"He was a tall guy with dark hair. Think he lost his hat stealing the horse. He was bareheaded."

"No one like that passed here today."

"Your man sick?"

"That's the Mexican, Juarez. He's been throwing up and has the bad bowels. Guess he's got *cockias*," she said.

"What's that?"

"Pretty contagious, they say—"

"Yeah, well, we were going on, ma'am. He ain't here. Let's ride." The half dozen men galloped away on their horses. The dust from their exit drifted across Slocum. Satisfied at last that they were gone, he sat up.

"My new name's now Juarez and I have the *cockias*?"

"Stupid men. How could a man steal a horse with his hands tied behind his back?" She stared hard in the direction they rode off in. "When did you eat last?"

"Two days ago."

"Oh my—" Her long fingers flew to her face and her eyes widened in disbelief. "Why didn't you say so before?"

"Ain't had time."

"Oh, my, I will fix you something—what will it be?" She searched about the camp as if in a quandary about what to prepare for him.

Her corn dodgers left from their morning meal chased with cool water from a canvas bag melted in his mouth. Heeding her precautions to eat his first meal slowly, he sat cross-legged and faced her.

Something about her drew him like a magnet; what he could do about it was another thing. No money, no gun, no horse, and miles from anything but Lordsburg and the greedy sheriff—there wasn't much he could do.

They both looked up at the approach of a wagon train.

He shook his head at her to dismiss any concern; they'd have no problems with such an outfit.

Long before they reached a place on the road opposite her camp, he heard the drivers' bullwhips pop and the creak of freight wagons eastward bound to the railroad's first shipping terminal in the East. Soon eighteen yokes of oxen hooked to doubles wagons snaked their way past on the road and the teamsters politely doffed their hats to Cyra in passing.

Late evening, Howard Ramsey and Coffee Brown returned with the repaired wagon wheel. All afternoon, she'd cooked pinto beans, with chunks of hog back, dried tomatoes and some red chilies, in the kettle over her fire for the evening meal.

With a sun-reddened face, Ramsey was a tall, rawboned man about thirty. He nodded and shook Slocum's hand. Coffee Brown had the innocent mask of a boy ten years younger than his age. His eagerness glinted out of his blue eyes, from behind his freckled nose.

"You the same Slocum they're looking for?" Ramsey asked.

"It was Jeb Dun yesterday. They finally got my name right?"

"Blacksmith told us two scruffy bounty hunters brought you in yesterday. You claiming they had the wrong man. Said you got away before they could hang you with that rapist. Said you damn sure took a good horse." Ramsey laughed. "Sounded like you had some real luck."

"Real close." Slocum shook his head. His wrists still burned, but Cyra's salve helped them.

"You want a job?" Brown asked.

"Doing what?"

"Laying track. They're hiring out here a couple of miles. Say they'll pay four bucks a day."

"Sounds high," Slocum said with a frown as Cyra

brought him a bowl of the steaming beans. He hoped his shrunken stomach kept it down.

"They can't get no one to work. Got all them Chinese working on the track coming from the west. Mines are all paying more. Coffee and I could use some more money before we go down there. They told us things was higher than hell in Tombstone anyway."

Slocum agreed with a nod. As he blew on his first spoonful, the rich smelling vapors from the beans ran up his nose and dazzled his brain. "Sure I'd go along. Need to do something."

"Be a day or two before you could do any work," Cyra said with a disapproving look at him.

"I'll recover fast on your good food." He raised his spoon at her in salute.

"Mister," Ramsey said, looking over as if appraising him. "I ain't certain about this whole deal at Lordsburg, you and that posse. But from that blacksmith's talk, you're a man that was falsely accused. But we better hitch up and get over into Arizona tonight, else you won't be doing any work for the railroad if that Lordsburg sheriff catches you."

"Good idea," Cyra said, looking up at him from stirring her beans with a big wooden spoon. "The sooner, the better."

After the meal, the teams were caught, and in the last of the sun's rays coming from somewhere beyond the distant Chiricahuas, they plodded their wagons and teams across the territorial line. As they made camp, a coyote yipped mournfully from a ridge above them. The sky was pricked with stars that cast a blue light across the great basin before them. Slocum appreciated his newfound friends' concern for his safety—and he felt better too to be in the Arizona Territory.

Animals were unhitched and turned out. Bedrolls being unfurled, Cyra came over and gave him an older ground cloth and a blanket to use. When she handed them to him, she gave a shrug as if that was the best she could do.

He thanked her and went to the far edge of the camp to spread them on the ground. Another sun dog yapped from the other direction, and that set off a chorus of their pitiful crying across the land.

"Hope them ain't so hungry they eat me," Brown said and rolled up in his blankets.

"Wouldn't want you," Ramsey said with a laugh. "Meat would be too stringy."

"Yeah, like shoe leather. Night."

The chorus of their good nights went around the camp and a coyote signed it off. Slocum wondered if he could even sleep, but soon his eyes shut and he drifted away.

In his hard slumber, he began to dream he was with Rosa again. She stood in the galvanized tub in the center of the room. Her short, rounded, ripe figure dripped streams of water. The smooth brown skin; her grapefruit-sized breasts, capped with large black nipples standing up like soldiers at attention; the slight swell to her stomach, indented by her navel, and the dark wet hair of her pubic area plastered to her—plenty of woman for him. She smiled and winked as he walked across the room with the towel to dry her.

First, he must dry her face, then he bent over and kissed her soft, full lips. Her small hands rubbed across the sides of his cheeks, tracing over his beard stubble. No time to towel her off, after he tasted the honey of her mouth. The need stirred in her body as he pressed his mouth even harder to meet hers.

Her tongue soon explored his teeth as he gathered her in his arms. The large globes pressed against his shirt, the same ones he had tasted and teased many times. That idea of sucking them made him grow heady at the recall of their firmness in his mouth.

Her fingers began to unbutton his shirt. He kissed her as if they were one and managed to dry her back in casual swipes, fully intrigued by the effect of their mouths glued together. Soon her small hands began to rub over the skin on his chest and sides.

Mouth to mouth, he numbly wiped the towel over her hips and upper legs, his thoughts entirely about lying on top of her. His hips ached to pound his dick into her. Exploring her smooth stomach, his hand soon sought her mound, combed through the stiff hair and she widened her stance for his entry between her legs. His middle finger riding the seam and then entered her. She gave a soft sigh and thrust her hips forward.

In an instant, she jerked loose his belt and the buttons on his fly so his pants fell to his bare feet and her hand soon pulled on his rising shaft.

Unable to contain himself, he swept her up and deposited her on the bed. Quickly he waded between her raised knees and used his hand to glide his erection inside her. In pleasure, she threw her head back at his entry and cried out loud. Then he looked down and saw that her throat was slashed, cut from side to side.

"Wake up! Wake up!" Cyra said aloud. "You must be dreaming!"

"Oh for God's sake—" He clutched her arms and sat up shaking like a man with the d.t.'s. Unable to control the tremors, he clenched his teeth tight, but they rattled like loose china dishes in a runaway wagon.

"Easy," she said and drew his face to the bodice of her dress. "It will pass. It will pass."

Slow-like, the involuntary muscles began to relax and the whole tenseness of the situation went from him like a mud slide into a creek. The slight flower scent of lavender clung to her and worked as a salve on his shattered mind. Her hugs became stronger, like a mother's. She gathered him away from the devil who had tried to steal him to that other world.

The other two had only looked up for a glance, then as if

satisfied she had matters in hand, they pulled up their so-gans and went back to sleep. He rested in her arms and it felt good. For a man without a dime, a gun, knife or horse, and only bad memories of his most recent past, he could cling to her for the rest of the night and forget all the rest.

"Sorry," he finally said and sat upright.

"No reason to be. We all have ghosts that come back to haunt us. For months after his death, I awoke, trying to stop him from bending over to check that mule's shoe." She shook her head with her long flowing hair past her shoulders. "I never got to him in time, no matter how hard I tried."

Slocum swallowed hard and nodded. "Never in time to save them."

"It must be our conscience blaming us." She gathered up her legs to sit cross-legged and covered herself with the skirt. "For what we could not have stopped at the time."

"I guess so."

"Will you rest a few days before you go take the rail-road job?"

"I better try to work."

"It will be hot and hard for you."

"I'll make it."

"You aren't a man to shirk, are you?"

"Try not to be."

"You have more story to tell than a mistaken identity."

"Perhaps, perhaps," he agreed with a nod, noting that even the coyotes had gone to roost. "Perhaps someday I can tell you."

"Not necessary. Now you will need your sleep. Will you be all right?"

"Yes, ma'am."

"Fine, I'll hope you can sleep anyway."

He helped her up and held her hands in his for a moment longer than brief. With them still in his grip, he nodded and thanked her. In the pearly starlight, she wet her lips then bobbed her head and pulled them free. "Good night."

3

"Any of you ever laid any track before?" the whiskered foreman O'Brien asked the three of them.

"We've worked teams, split posts, built fence, done mechanic work like build houses. How hard can track laying be?" Ramsey asked.

"It is. Trust me, lads, it's the hardest job in the world." The gray-bearded man, who looked like a leprechaun to Slocum as he addressed them, wore a dirt-soiled, green checkered suit and a derby hat with a gold watch chain that ran across his potbelly.

"Well, ya can start packing rails. Eight men, four to the side, and you carry your share. Don't drop them. Man loses his toes doing that. Ain't yours that's lost, then the other guy might carve one off you for dropping it on his."

"Pays four bucks a day?" Ramsey asked.

"Yeah, if you make it that long."

The three of them went over to report to Dunagan, a bear of a man, who wore no shirt and whose sun-blackened chest was floured with dust.

"Get ahold of them tongs," Dunagan said. "When I say lift, then you do your part."

Slocum noticed that several of the workers were

Apache or Mexican, with some hard-eyed whites. The three of them assumed a place on the left.

"Lift!" came the command and they all bent over and hoisted up the twelve feet of rail. No small task, Slocum soon learned.

"Forward!" Dunagan shouted and they proceeded toward the fresh ties stretching ahead.

"Set down!" Dunagan ordered.

The Apache on Slocum's right grinned big. "Know you."

"Yeah, my name is—"

"Big Horse," the Apache said in his tongue. "Mary Burns say you have dick like a big stallion." He began to laugh at his own joke and shake his head.

"What's that Injun funnying you about?" Ramsey demanded as they walked the ties, going back for the next rail.

"Nothing," Slocum said to put down the man's upset. This would be a long day; they didn't need any trouble. "He's laughing about an old deal."

They lifted each rail, proceeded to the place needed, and set it down, all day in the blistering sun. Slocum began to recall Mary Burns: the lithe, willowy figure in swirling buckskin and beads; her stomp dancing in the light of a great piñon fire; black eyes and lashes flashing at him, then turning away as if she was opening and closing the canvas flap on her wickiup for the white man who skinned mules for General Crook.

No doubt a widow, the story of her lost warrior went untold since Apaches never spoke of their dead. He could remember that night in the White Mountains when he met her. Long after other dancers had collapsed, she came to where he stood in their shadows, his back to a ponderosa trunk, arguing with himself if he should go back to camp or watch more of the dancing.

"Come," she said sharply. "They tell me white men are

only half as big as good Indians. I want to see yours."

"Maybe a quarter as long," he said with a laugh and let her drag him into the timbers' deep darkness.

"So let me see yours," she said, holding both of his hands and leaning back.

"He can't appear by magic."

"Oh." She let go of his hands and squeezed her chin in the starlight filtering down upon them.

He undid his belt and then undid the buttons. His pants fell to his knees in the inky black seclusion of the forest, with the turpentine smell deep in his nose. What could she see?

In a flash, she was before him. He could smell her strong musk and felt her long fingers gently stroke the length of his dick. Then as if not satisfied, she pulled on it ever so smoothly. Her attention caused it to rise, and she swallowed loud, like a big fish splashing water in the night.

"How much Indian are you?" she asked slyly.

"Enough to enjoy you."

"Oh, it is too big for me."

"Never. We can go slow."

"I am not certain. It is very big."

"Why did you ask then?" he demanded angrily, feeling that she had only dragged him out there to tease him. In that case, he would go back to the mule camp.

When he bent for his pants, she stayed his hands. "You will go very slow?"

"I can."

"I will get ready for you," she said and knelt on the ground. On all fours, she glanced back up at him. He could barely make out her silhouette, but he dropped to his knees. Her actions had begun an erection. So he raised her skirt higher onto her back to expose the half moons of her butt. His hands ran over the smooth skin, feeling the firmness of her muscular butt, satisfied that what lay ahead would be of great pleasure for him. He waded up until his belly was against her, then he eased the nose of his dick between her legs. She reached under and started the nose into her lubricated slot.

The way was tight. When the aching head of his erection reached her ring, he began to gently pump against the restriction. Only a small portion of the glans could start into the round, muscular opening. Then their fluids began to flow. He gripped her shoulders, and with his butt driving it, he shoved his dick past the tight circle. Her quick cry stabbed him, but they were one, and the passion of their connection turned into a wild ride.

He reached around in front and found her stiff clit. His fingertip rubbed the stubby knob until soon she began moaning. Both short of breath, they fought on. Then the pangs of fire shot through his butt and he gave a final deep plunge. The fountain of come shot out the head of his dick in blinding pleasure, and they collapsed in a pile.

"How is Mary?" he asked the man in Apache as they walked back bearing another rail.

"She's a whore at the mines," he said.

Slocum nodded that he had heard the man. No matter what mines he meant, she no doubt had fallen into alcoholism and the easy money. Who would wait in a wickiup for the government allotments of wormy flour and cornmeal, rancid grease and skinny longhorn beef, tougher than old shoe leather? Go and screw the miners, Mary, and drink whiskey until you can forget the old days. Those days were gone forever when she had a man who would love her, fiercely bring her fresh game, and barter for new wheat and corn. The proud one could trade for cotton material from the Mexican traders for her, so she could make new dresses, or he would hunt for the deer skins she used to make her special fringed clothing for stomps.

"Set down!" Dunagan shouted. They obeyed, and the

rail in place, Slocum and the others headed back for a water break. One of the few moments of rest in their tiring day under the glaring sun was when the workers swigged the alkali water from wooden barrels that someone filled out of some murky water source.

After dark, they rode the team horses back to camp, where Cyra had food ready for them. They barely forced it down and fell like dead men into their blankets. Such days would be their life: up before dawn, at the end of the tracks by daylight, ready for work, carrying rails forward to be spiked down on the pitch-smelling ties. O'Brien soon assigned Ramsey to a slip and a team of mules on the fill crew. The iron dirt slip they called a fresno. You lifted the handles, clucked to the mules and forced the blade into the dirt until full, then you drove the mules up on the grade they were building. When the fresno was where the foreman indicated he wanted it, the driver raised the handles and clucked to the mules again, and they dumped the earth by tipping the boat over. Once the boat was empty, the driver had to flip it back and return for more.

In the white powdery dust of the Arizona desert, it proved a dirt-chocking job that forced Ramsey to wear a bandanna over his face to filter part of it out. He came home each night floured with it, and for a lack of available water, the three were unable to bathe, so dead tired after the meal they fell on their blankets and slept.

"We have to find more water than what we drink," Cyra complained toward the end of the second week. "We all need a bath and I need to wash."

Slocum agreed. "Sunday, we can drive to a creek. You can wash clothes there and we can all clean up."

"How far away is it?"

"Maybe twenty miles, but there's water there."

"Oh, thank God," she said and dropped her chin with a wary shake of he head.

The next day at work, the Apache asked Slocum if he wanted a house.

"Where?"

"Ahead," he motioned with a slight toss of his braided hair.

"How far?"

"Maybe two miles," the Apache said and shrugged as if it was only a short ways there. Then Slocum recalled the nickname that the scouts called him, Constipated.

"There's a deserted adobe ahead." He gave a toss of his sombrero-shaded head.

"Which way?"

"Go to the big wash and ride up it. You will see the old corrals." He threw up his right hand to indicate the side.

"Who does it belong to?"

"Gone." He shook his head with a deadpan expression on his sun-black face.

"Why?"

"When this was Chiricahua land, the agent Jeffords made them get out."

Slocum nodded. During the next water break, he told Brown he would have to check on the place after work, so for Brown and Ramsey to go back to camp and he would be along later. All day, his mind was on some place of her own. A woman always did better in a house.

When they quit for the day, in the setting sun he jumped on the thin work horse's back and trotted him westward. In a short while, he reached the sandy dry wash and turned the animal northward. As Constipated promised, he discovered the old corrals first and rode up on a trail from under the steep cut bank. It wasn't much more than a hovel; the hitch rail was broken, and the chicken pen long ago fallen in. A few mesquite trees and two straggly cottonwoods shaded the place. Ideal, he decided. There must be a well somewhere. He had dismounted and started to go though the front door to inspect—when the dry rattle beside his leg made him freeze. No knife and no gun.

In the last glow of the sunset, he dared to carefully step back one and then two measured steps until he at last found himself outside, unscathed, and his heart began to pump again. For a long while, he stood at the broken-down hitch rack and regained his breath. So there were some rattlers here too that wanted to share the place. He better mention them to everyone. An old abandoned place like this made a great home for such rodent hunters.

Satisfied, he swung on the high-backboned horse. "Mr. Snake, go find you a new home or you will die." He saluted the small hovel with his hand and sent the work horse in a trot for Cyra's camp.

"How nice is it? How big? When can I see it?" she asked, excited as a child at Christmas when he returned to camp.

"As soon as we can get a day off or Sunday."

She collapsed her hands in her lap. "I don't think I can wait."

"Oh, yes, it won't be long."

"If you were tired as I am, you could wait a long time," Brown said and fell over on his blankets.

The others laughed.

"Oh, Slocum, I am so excited I won't be able to sleep."

"Try. It will be lots of work, it's run down. I never found the well either."

"There should be one?"

"Should," he agreed and went back to eating his supper. This rail carrying job had found new muscles in his body to ache, but he was becoming tougher to it by the day. He agreed with her, a bath would be wonderful. His dirt-stiff pants had chaffed raw the insides of his legs and crotch. Whew.

•   •   •

Sunday, they loaded and hitched two teams to each wagon and began the trek. Even at dawn, thick clouds were gathering down in Mexico, and Slocum wondered if they wouldn't finally get an afternoon monsoonal shower. Each afternoon, the thunderstorm had been over the Chiricahuas and mountains to the south, but had missed them. The thunder rolled across the valley like cannon fire, and every so often a cool gush of air that smelled of wet pine and juniper needles came on the wind.

"I'd stand in that rain all day if it would just come," Brown said.

"Maybe, maybe not," Slocum said. "It gets cold fast."

"I'd love to be cold just once."

So after they left the end of the rails, they drove up between the staked right-of-way wagon tracks and finally turned up the dry wash. Slocum drove the first wagon, with Cyra on the seat beside him.

"How much further?" she asked.

"A mile or so is all."

"Can we file on it?"

"I guess."

"You don't sound like you like this idea." She turned and frowned at him.

"I can't say how long I can stay here."

He glanced over and saw her understanding nod. "I know. I knew it the day I found you. There was more than you told me, wasn't there?"

"Yes. And I may have to leave anytime soon."

She reached over and squeezed his knee. "Don't tell me, just go."

"I will."

"This rattlesnake in my house?"

"Guess he's the first one we have to evict. You see this wash?" He nodded his head toward the flat, sandy bed they drove up.

"Yes."

"If it ever rains up in the north, this will flood and become an angry river. Don't try to cross it."

She nodded obediently.

"It'll be a bad one. It can come up without warning too. You must respect it."

"I will. If we get everything done here, will you take me to the Chiricahuas and the creek next Sunday?"

Slocum turned and smiled at her. "Yes, I will."

"Good." She clapped him on the knee and winked at him confidentially. "A house will make a difference—for all of us. You'll see."

Mid-morning, they pulled the rigs up on the high bank and surveyed the place. Hands on their hips, both Brown and Ramsey walked around the jacal armed with large ironwood sticks selected to thump rattlers on the head. An hour later, they had a half dozen dead sidewinders hanging on the chicken fence made of ocotillo stems. With long knives, the men cut the tall bunchgrass back from the house, along with the weeds and brush.

Slocum found the well, moved back the slab rocks over it and dropped a pail on a rope into the water below. He hoisted the first one up, smelled it and declared it fit to drink. They shared two gourds and sipped the product, nodding and agreeing.

"That old stone trough looks like it will hold water," Ramsey said and tossed some posts out of it, being careful not to uncover another diamondback.

By dark, they had all taken a bath, washed their clothing and watered the eight horses, who acted pleased to be eating the bunchgrass around the place.

While Cyra took her bath in the trough, the men went around in front and repaired the corral to contain three of the horses they would ride to the end of the track the next day. Cyra would get up three more the next afternoon, and they would be on hand for them to ride the following morning. That gave each animal a chance to recover, though they could graze all day with hobbles while the men worked. Slocum could see the horses were healing and gaining weight. He wondered if the other two men realized how close they had been to being without animals. Mules were always better than horses. Could do more and take more, but what man ever liked a damn stubborn, hardheaded jackass more than he did a horse? Some liked mules better, but not many, and the death of Cyra's husband no doubt had tempered their choices.

"Could we run cattle?" Ramsey asked.

"Sure. Now they've got the Apaches gone from here. A man could build himself a ranch here."

"What would we need?" Brown asked, putting the last stick in the pile system that made the corral.

"A brand, some cows and a bull."

"How hard is the brand to get?"

"Ride to Tucson and register one is what I know about it."

"How much will it cost?"

"Maybe ten dollars to register it. Any blacksmith will make you an iron for two bucks."

"So we need twelve dollars. Those loose cattle out there I've seen in the brush that have no brand on them?" Ramsey asked.

"They're yours to brand, if you have a registered brand on this range."

"Free!" Brown shouted.

"Free to rope," Slocum said, seeing that neither man had ever tried to capture wild cattle in his life. It wasn't much worse than laying track every day, but they weren't simply for free.

"How far is Tucson from here?" Brown asked, excitement shining in his eyes.

"Sixty miles. Take a couple of days to get there and back, huh?" Ramsey said, shaking his head as if overwhelmed.

"I'd say five, six days all together for a round trip," Slocum offered.

"Could we file a claim on this too?" Brown asked.

"Sure, if we can look at the railroad map and figure out the location."

"Yeah, but the four of us could file on four places, couldn't we?" Brown asked.

"Sure, but I would claim this one first, then find some live water at each one and get a claim with water on it. No one will want the grazing land in between the claims."

"Can you show us how to brand and all that? We'd help you strike a claim too."

Slocum shook his head. "I'll help the three of you."

"But why don't you—"

Cyra came around the house in a fresh dress, looking spanking new, and interrupted Brown. "Let Slocum alone. He's got his things to do."

"Sure, doggone, why Cyra, you sure look nice." Brown blinked at his discovery.

"It's going to be a lot better for all of us with a house."

"And some ranches," Ramsey added and nodded his head in approval.

Thunder in the southwest increased and the looming thunderheads began to pile up over the Chiricahuas. Slocum studied them. Those storms were about to bust free of those mountains with all the force they had.

"We better get her four-poster bed set up and that tarp stretched over it in a hurry," Slocum said, disturbed that they might not have time to set it up before the downburst struck them.

"The roof going to leak?" Brown asked in disbelief.

"All Mexican roofs leak. It just does not rain much, so why fix them?" Slocum laughed as they hurried. The bed was soon up, and the feather mattress installed. The men stretched the tarpaulin over it as a puff of dust and the first smell of rain swept across the valley and in the front door.

"Damn, I'll stay out in it till hell freezes over," Brown said and rushed outside to breast the first onslaught of water and wind.

An hour later, the four of them sat cross-legged on Cyra's bed. Water ran off the tarp into buckets, and the rain slashed at the outside walls. The air was fresh with the smell of wet grass and creosote; the lightning blinded them, then thunder rolled over the leaking roof like a cannon wagon full of loose balls.

"Hell finally froze over," Brown said, looking at the soaked Ramsey hugging his arms.

"Never thought it would be that cold."

They laughed.

4

If dirt was bad, mud proved worse. O'Brien took several
crew members back toward Lordsburg by the work train
to shore up a threatened bridge over a flooded wash. The
engine and cars backed over it, leaving timbers on the
tracks for them to reenforce the structure being challenged
by the bank-to-bank surge of raging brown water. The
crew swarmed over the bridge attempting to strap more
timbers to the legs. With a coil of heavy rope across his
shoulder, Slocum was over the side standing on a crosspiece, the muddy water swirling around him, while the
others eased down a big pole for him to tie to the leg.
Leery about this patchwork, he knew if the force of the
water ever caught it, the whole structure would be swept
away.

"Get a rope around it!" the Irishman shouted at him
through his hands.

Slocum nodded. His life wasn't worth the damn pole.
If it started to go, he wasn't going with it and that potbellied Irishman in his muddy green checkered suit could
do it himself, if he didn't like how Slocum worked it.

Roaring water sounds in his ears, and his footing pre-
carious on the cross beam, he had no idea—then the

cracking noises began. The whole damn bridge began to lurch downstream.

Men began to shout. "Run for your lives!"

Slocum looked up, and above him Brown was on his belly extending a hand down to pull him up. His hand clasped Brown's forearm, and the crosspiece under him began to give way. He glanced down for a second at the boiling water rising to his waist, sucking at him as he attempted to pull himself up. Then Constipation's handsome copper face shone from above as he too reached for Slocum. They pulled him up. On his knees, at last on the bridge, he could feel the rise and the twisting of the structure underneath him.

"Come on! Come on!" Brown screamed and started for the western side.

Constipation ran ahead of them. The ties began to pitch, buckle and roll like a ship at sea. As Slocum hurried to escape the collapse, he glanced over his shoulder. The far bank where O'Brien and the others had gone looked a mile away. He only caught sight of their backs going the other way. The ties before them buckled and then the whole thing dropped down into the water. His water-sodden boots struck every fifth tie in his long stride, and he hoped one didn't come loose under his weight as they ran harder and harder.

Where were the other men? Had they reached safety on the other side? He could see the Apache ahead of him. Slocum blinked, then he realized that the Apache had stripped to his breechcloth, his brown legs churning like a steam engine piston. Then the surface of the ties dropped down again and swung sideways. They ran uphill, and Slocum knew the bridge had given in the middle of the stream and they'd be lucky not to be taken away with it.

Both he and Brown gave a final burst and reached the bank—out of breath, their strength gone. They spilled off the fill and rolled down the muddy slope. At the base they looked at each other in disbelief. Coated in brown mud from head to toe, they were alive and hugged each other.

"Where's Constipation?" Slocum asked, finally looking all around.

"Up here. I never liked that mud," the Apache said. Standing in his breechcloth, feet apart above them on the tracks, the Indian smiled and laughed.

Slocum shook his head—too close for comfort. He began the slick climb up the steep slope, offering a hand to Brown, who shook his head with a "I'll make it."

On top at last, Slocum looked around. "Where's that Irishman?"

"O'Brien?" Constipation asked.

"Yeah, I don't see him or the others." He used his hands to shield his eyes to see better.

"They ran the other way."

"They ain't over there, are they?" Slocum asked, squinting his eyes to look across the gaping space of churning brown water at the far bank.

The Apache's head shook no.

"Could they swim?" Brown asked puzzled.

"I doubt it." Slocum wet his cracked lips. The foreman wouldn't be the first or the last man to die in a dry-wash flood on a cloudless day.

"There's six more men missing besides him." Brown said. "We were all there when the bridge buckled—"

Slocum drew a deep breath and nodded. Seven men had paid the price with their lives, and they weren't even halfway across the valley yet.

John Ripple was the railroad supervisor. He crossed the receding stream late that afternoon on horseback, a tall, clean-shaven man under a wide-brim hat and wearing a dark suit. His pant legs were stained brown from where the water sought them. He dismounted where Slocum,

Brown and the Apache sat waiting the turn of event.

"Where is O'Brien?" he asked.

"Him and six more went downstream when the bridge broke," Brown said, standing up and brushing at the dried mud on his clothing.

"You three all right?"

"So far, sir," Slocum said and rose up from his seat on the rail. "Not much we could do until the water went down."

"I wasn't worried about that. You men will be paid for a full day."

"Good enough, sir."

"The day is nearly finished. Let's meet back here in the morning. We will have to make an attempt to find the bodies then. By then the water will be down enough, I suppose."

"It should be, sir."

"Your name?"

"Slocum. That's Brown and he's Apache."

"He doesn't have a name?" The man blinked and checked his horse.

"You couldn't say it if he told you. The troopers called him Constipated, but he likes Apache just fine, sir."

Amused, Ripple nodded. "I agree. With those choices, I'd be Apache too."

"He likes it."

Apache nodded.

"Then you men have tents or camps?" He looked around as if to spot them.

"We do. We'll report here in the morning?"

With a disgusted look at the damage, Ripple turned back and agreed. "Good thing that the locomotive and work train got over there before it went. But we can't build another mile of track without them over here on this side. Damn floods—what a mess."

"Should we bring the teamsters and others here tomorrow to make the search?" Slocum asked.

"Yes, what is your first name?"

"John, but they call me Slocum."

"Yes. You, Slocum, are the man in charge of the west bank and the search. Tell them all to report to you here."

"I'll handle it, sir."

"Very good," he said as he mounted, then he turned his horse back to the stream. The light-footed animal went down the fill bank, and after Ripple spurred him twice, he moved into the water, then headed for the far bank.

"Got us a new boss, Injun," Brown said.

"Good thing too."

"Why's that?"

"We not save him, there'd been lots of Apache women cried, 'cause we let that big-dicked bastard drown today." Apache laughed aloud until Brown joined him in his mirth.

At last, with tears in his eyes, Brown clapped Apache on the shoulder. "Been a big waste, huh?"

And they laughed again.

Slocum gave them a disapproving head shake. In midstream, Ripple's good horse stepped off into a washout in the ford and was forced to swim some, so the man's fine pants would be muddy to the crotch. At last, though, Slocum could see that Ripple had successfully recrossed the river.

"Let's go to hiking," he said to the two others, and they started home.

"Seven men lost today?" Cyra asked as she dished them out tin plates heaping with her bean dish.

"Could have been more," Slocum said. "We were on a fool's mission. Those extra poles they wanted lashed on wouldn't have held nothing."

"Didn't make any sense to me," Brown agreed, ready to dig in and eat.

"Will you find their bodies?" Cyra asked, going about filling coffee cups.

"Maybe, maybe not," Slocum said. "They could be buried under all the silt and mud. No telling."

"So you're the new boss?" she asked, looking at Slocum as she bent over to pour Ramsey's cup.

"To find the bodies is all."

With a whimsical toss of her head and smirk that he could see in the firelight, she said, "I hope you like the position."

"I been figuring, we—she needs some supplies," Ramsey said as if in deep thought between bites about the trip to Tucson. "After this week, we would have like forty-three dollar apiece coming, plus my extra buck a day as a teamster. That's over a hundred dollars,"

"Now wait," she said taking a seat. "Slocum may have other things—"

"Let him go on," Slocum said to her.

"Well, that we would buy the brand, the iron, some supplies, tools enough, canvas to line the roof, and we could mud coat it and stop the rain coming in."

"All I want for my share," Slocum said, "is a cheap saddle, say ten bucks should buy an old hull for me to ride. A cap-and-ball Navy .44—that will cost two bucks—and some ammunition for it. The rest you can put in the pot for supplies."

"I guess we'll need three saddles if we aim to round up cattle," Ramsey said.

"Need some rope to catch them," Brown said.

Cyra chimed in too. "Coffee, beans, baking powder, cans of tomatoes, a few peaches, flour, lard, raisins and sugar." Using her fingers, she listed everything for Ramsey.

"Who should go?" he asked.

"You," they said in unison.

"Then it's settled." he said. "I'll haul out for Tucson Sunday morning."

"You have a gun?" Slocum asked.

"Shotgun."

"Keep it loaded and handy all the way coming and going. There is more riffraff traveling this road than ever before. They ever learn that you're packing a hundred dollars on you, why they'd cut your throat like that." Slocum snapped his fingers. "Don't tell a soul on the job either about this mission. Bunch of them are sure enough hard cases."

"We're all going to be secret," Brown agreed.

"I'll sew it inside his vest," Cyra said.

"Good idea." Slocum looked at the red-hot ashes stirred by the gentle night wind and wondered.

"How many bodies we gonna find in the morning?" Ramsey asked as if still in deep thought between bites. He shook his head to try to clear it.

Slocum filled with dread as he watched the sunset burn the last of the daylight in an orange-purple flair. Be sure enough a grim task for them.

A dozen men armed with long sticks, barefooted and pants legs rolled up, stood on the bank. The stream was down to a few feet wide, of light brown sludge flowing southward. Here and there, the silver glimpse of water was strung through the flow. The hundred-yard-wide strip of drying mud already smelled sour.

"Spread out. Put your stick into any large lump or mound. The bodies won't be lying out in the open. They've been rolled in this stuff. Spread out. Each man take his part," Slocum ordered. Shoes strung around their necks, they began the march.

On the bank, Ripple rode his light-footed horse and Ramsey drove a farm wagon with mules hitched for an ambulance. Slocum had stocked it with a roll of fresh canvas to wrap the corpses in.

"Check those side places," he shouted to some men on the edges sauntering down the wash.

The first mile produced nothing. Slocum found who were the laggards and prodded them verbally to check more drifts. Then he saw vultures circling in the sky. He began to hasten his pace.

"You all keep checking; that might only be a dead cow." He saw Ripple standing in the stirrups in a military pose that he'd suspected from the first the man would know—ex-military, anyway. The soft mud was dry enough not to cling to his feet, and Slocum ran the last hundred yards to see several of the large black birds reluctantly rise up in flight.

"Body number one," he said under his breath. Then, at the gunshot, he swiveled around. Ripple had taken down a buzzard on the wing, and the black bird crashed in the stream, flopped in the mud and puked, before it went limp.

"Know him?" Ripple asked, reining up his dancing horse beside the muddy form.

"Called himself John Smith," Slocum said, recognizing, even under the mud coating, the hard-faced man who bedded ties.

"John Smith one or two?" Ripple asked, looking in his book.

"The others will know."

"John Smith anyway," he said and wrote that in his book with a pencil.

Slocum looked toward Ramsey on the bank, but he was already cutting off a sheet of cloth to wrap the dead man in. The sun was high enough that it began to bore down on them, and the rising humidity added to their discomfort. Somewhere out in the head-high brush, a quail called and its mate answered.

Slocum looked back at the men. "Keep searching. There could be other bodies hidden."

Noontime, they had found four of them. One was stretched over a treetop, another under a pile of muddy sand, another with his arms outstretched, looking at the sun, as clean as if he'd been washed for his funeral.

Slocum went ahead while the men took a break. A hundred yards downstream, he spotted two men with horses. They were bent over something. Then in the distance he saw them lift an object that shone like gold in the sun. O'Brien's watch. They were grave robbers.

"Put that down!" he shouted through his cupped hands.

His words were only spurs to them, for they hastily mounted and charged away. Slocum reached for his gun and realized halfway there that he wore none. But Ripple did, and he had a horse that could catch them.

Over the slick mud floor, Slocum raced. Out of breath, he stopped before the man.

"Your pistol and horse," he gasped. "No time for explanations. They're getting away."

Ripple blinked and handed him the single-action Colt by the butt first. Slocum jammed it in his waistband and, in a bound, was horseback and discovering the big bay was a winner. They flew over the stream and in an instant were on top of the next rise.

Obviously the pair expected no pursuit from a man on foot. They were trotting their horses across the wide flat headed east. Slocum sent the bounding horse after them, clearing small washes as if with wings.

His appearance startled the two, and they began whipping their shaggy mounts, but it was to no avail. The great bay closed the distance in no time, and Slocum had the Colt in his fist. He fired a round over their heads. Obviously a little shy at the percussion, the bay ducked to the left, but Slocum held his seat as both men reined up and threw their hands in the air.

"Who's got that watch?" he demanded.

The two breeds looked at each other in disbelief.

"I want O'Brien's gold watch. Now!"

"Here!" the younger one said and hoisted it by the chain from his pants pocket. Neither of them was armed, but Slocum felt they should be turned over to Ripple and let him decide their fate.

He rode in and jerked the watch away from the boy. "Now head back, and we'll see what the Southern Pacific wants to do with grave robbers."

"It wasn't no grave," one of them mumbled.

"Just as well have been," Slocum said and waved the gun muzzle for them to move out.

Halfway across the basin, he saw that all the men were lined across the ridge, clapping and shouting. He shook his head, then wiggled his mud-drying bare feet in the stirrups as the bay horse danced along behind the other two. The day wasn't over yet either.

5

They never found the seventh man's body. Six neat graves lay in a row on the south side of the tracks west of the shattered bridge that workers swarmed over to replace. Ripple decided to take the two prisoners back to Lordsburg and show them the jail for thirty days. A railroad held many prerogatives and solutions to anyone who committed a crime against them; thirty days in jail was an easy one to attain for troublemakers. The two robbers were sent back as prisoners with a work crew.

"Slocum, I knew you were a commander the first day I set eyes on you." A sly smile appeared on Ripple's face as the two prepared to part. "You can line up the rest of the supplies over here tomorrow and give me an inventory. Anything you wish?"

"Yes, a map of the tracks ahead," Slocum said.

"That's my man. Know where you are going," Ripple said with an air of superior approval. "I'll have you one in the morning."

"Thanks. Good night, sir."

"Good night, Slocum, and thanks for the job well done today." Ripple stood up in the saddle and set the bay off the bank, then loped him across the almost dry wash.

"What do you need a map for?" Ramsey asked, leading up Slocum's horse for him. "You plan on becoming a permanent employee?"

"No," Slocum said and then searched around to be certain they were alone. "To find the section number we need to file that claim on her ranch."

Ramsey laughed aloud. "You had me worried. I thought for a minute that you'd gone soft on this new boss job."

Bellied over the tall horse, Slocum straightened on his back and scooted up on his withers. "Not yet, I haven't." The three of them headed for the ranch.

"New supervisor?" she asked, when Slocum returned from his bath. He dried his hair with a towel, standing beneath the remada they had fixed for her to cook under. It was a shade set on poles with lots of brush and weeds piled on top to cut the sun and let the wind through, a place where she could fix her food and even take a nap in a hammock. The red of the fire reflected off her face. Some of the strains that had marked her looks that first day had faded, despite the hard efforts she put out each day to draw water for the horses and clean up more around the site; the house was a good place for her. She, like their livestock, was fast mending.

"Just a job." He shrugged away her obvious excitement.

"What does it pay?"

"He never said. More than carrying rails, I'd bet."

"He even caught some thieves that stole a watch off a dead man," Brown said, getting around the kettles on the fire to fill his tin plate.

She glanced at Slocum with a questioning look.

"Nothing. They'd stole O'Brien's watch. I saw them and they ran off."

"He got Ripple's horse and took his gun and went after them two like a house on fire."

"They were just some young breeds."

"Aw, way I seen it, you had to shoot at them to get them to stop. We were all up there watching." Brown shook his head. "It sure impressed the hell out of me."

"This job that you all have sure is exciting," she said and fished a browned biscuit out of the dutch oven. Tossing it from hand to hand to cool, she looked off in the night as a coyote howled. "Got plenty of them out here. Maybe we ought to brand them?"

"Be a coyote rancher?" Ramsey asked, looking up from the plate in his lap.

"Yeah, be different." She smiled at them and shook her head. "Just a thought."

"When you go to Tucson, Ramsey, go by the doc and ask if he knows what possesses a woman to want to coyote ranch," Slocum said with wide grin.

"If you think I'm going to water your cows with a bucket out of that well, you three better think again," she said and took a small bite from the biscuit.

"Better buy a pitcher pump and some pipe then too," Slocum said.

"I hope we've got enough money for all your wants and needs." Ramsey shook his head as if frustrated by the new order.

"All that money the new boss'll make should cover it," Brown said.

"That ain't fair—" She gave them a peevish look.

"It's fair, I'm in this with the three of you."

"Well, all right, but the way you all are wearing out the clothes on your backs, you may be wearing nothing."

"Some waist overalls," Ramsey said aloud. "For the three of us."

"Shirts too," she said, still nibbling on the biscuit.

"You eating?" Slocum asked.

"Sure. I simply wanted to enjoy this biscuit, 'cause there ain't much baking powder left and my sourdough liquor died two weeks ago."

"If you have some lard and flour left, guess we can have tortillas."

"You can make them?" she asked Slocum.

"I'm not great at it, but I can make them something like the Mexicans do."

"After supper, you show me how," she said, acting excited.

"I will." He met her look and nodded.

The tortilla lesson went well, and the other two nodded in approval at the taste test. Cyra soon was able to make them in her hands, patting them into thin white discs, tossing them on a hot skillet and flipping them with her fingers. Freckled with some burned spots, they made perfect ones and she laughed.

"Now you must call me señora."

"If we don't get to sleep," Ramsey said, "the new boss may not make it up in time."

They laughed. Then the men rose wearily and shook out their bedrolls, in case some varmint like a scorpion or other desert vermin had taken residence in them.

A round of "good nights" and they covered up. By dawn, the heat of the day would be evaporated and a chill would awaken the uncovered sleeper with his teeth chattering.

She roused them in the predawn to feed them fried mush, cold biscuits and hot coffee. They soon caught their horses in the corral and rode off for the work camp with a wave for her.

Slocum spoke to the surveyor first thing, a young man who wore glasses and looked fresh out of some Eastern college in his baggy pants and button-up sweater. Terrance Gould was the youth's name.

"How is the grade building coming?" Slocum asked.

"We should be further out in front of the track laying. Piling dry material up like this without a chance to settle is not what I was taught as proper roadbed construction."

"You ever tell that to O'Brien?"

"He said, the hell with the way I was taught, they had a blankety-blank railroad to build."

"I can imagine," Slocum agreed. "I'll have the teamsters back at their fill work today. Maybe I can get Ripple to do what you suggest. Losing that bridge was severe enough that the upper management may want to listen."

"Tell me something, Slocum."

"What's that?"

"Why in God's name did those Apaches fight so hard for this godforsaken land?"

" 'Cause it was theirs."

"I guess so, but it sure is dry out here unless it rains, and then it floods—there's no in between. I'd've let them had it."

Slocum nodded. The young man would probably never see the islands in the sky like the Chiricahuas and the Dragoons. Never see the splendor of those pine forests and cool breezes that washed one's face, drink from the cold springs that sprung out of rocks. Never would he know why the Apaches loved the land; all he would ever see would be the dust and desolation.

With Brown busy inventorying ties, Slocum sent the rest of the track crew ahead to clear brush on the right-of-way. It was still early when Ripple arrived. Slocum and Brown were counting plates and spikes.

"How's things this morning?" he asked, dismounting.

"We're working. Teamsters are hauling fill. What's left of the track crew's cutting brush on the right-of-way. Brown and I about have the inventory completed."

"Good. Let's take a minute and talk." Ripple gave him a head toss and they walked aside, with the supervisor leading his horse.

Out of earshot of Brown, Ripple stopped. "You're a wanted man in New Mexico."

"Is that bad?"

"No, considering you escaped a vigilante hanging."

"You want me to leave?"

"No. You wanted in Arizona?"

"Not that I know about."

"Good. Don't ride the train back to New Mexico is all."

"I won't. I spoke to that young surveyor. Figure he's got more education than anything, but he says he's been opposed to building on this fresh dry fill and O'Brien said to hell with his concern."

Ripple nodded. "It's risky, but we have such limited time and funds. That bridge we lost was only temporary. How many rains like that do you have in ten years out here?"

"Not many."

"When we get the track completed, we can come back and build it right. That'll save us precious days. Maybe months. However, seven men gave their lives. Sorry, it's the way we have to push or there never would be any railroads built."

"What do they want me for in New Mexico besides that horse I rode out on?"

"Jailbreaking." Ripple became amused. He slapped his leg with his reins. "They might indict some locals with you as accomplice on that charge. Sorry, it must not have been funny, coming that close to being hung."

"Anyone find the horse?"

Ripple shook his head. "Still must be running away."

"I ain't see him again either. That's the way you want it, I'll start back laying track in the morning."

"We'll be bringing the supplies out by wagons. I hired some more men until the bridge is fixed and the work train can get out here."

"More men?"

"I'll send a half dozen to be out here in the morning."

"Fine, sir."

"Where do you live?"

"Four miles west and two miles up a dry wash, at an old ranch place. Three of us stay there."

"Good. If I ever need you, then I'll know to find you there?"

"More than likely."

"Good luck, laying track." The man remounted his horse.

"I'll need it," Slocum said after him.

Ripple rode back toward the bridge project and Slocum went to find the tie bedding crew. They were bunched up at some sun-browned tents. A man with a pipe stepped out and introduced himself as Joyce—Bart Joyce.

"You think you can boss us?" The man jabbed his pipe stem at Slocum to punctuate his words. The others behind the man looked ready to spring upon him. Decision time— this crew of broad-shouldered emigrants needed to know who ran this track laying crew.

Slocum's hand shot out, caught a fistful of Joyce's shirt. He jerked the man to within inches of his face, so he could smell the strong tobacco flavor on his breath.

"Listen here, you don't want that pipe stuck up your ass, you better know who's running this crew. Me. My name's Slocum, and you don't like it, get the hell out of here—you savvy?"

"Yeah. Yeah. No need to get all mad."

"Good." Slocum released him and gave him enough of a push to make him step back into the others. "Why in the hell ain't you setting ties?"

"We're going." Joyce managed a hard swallow and with a head toss took the men with him.

"We ain't paying you to stand around either," he shouted after them.

Brown came over with a rather shocked look on his face. "How many of these crews you ran?"

"You mean how many have I worked on?" Slocum set

a smile in the corners of his mouth. "You just have to get your bluff in. Then it goes smoother."

Brown nodded. "Want me to pack these plates up on the track?"

Slocum nodded. He would need some sort of a payroll list when Ripple got back in the morning. Considering the task, he unrolled the map the man had brought him. It showed the next ten miles of right-of-way. He followed it to the bridge marked for their dry wash, then north. Where the wash turned to the northwest, he pointed to the spot with his finger—section nine would be the one they needed. He checked the range and the latitude. Ramsey could easily file on it with all that information.

Pleased with his discovery, he rolled up the map. Better go check on the right-of-way crew workers. He wondered how that Irishman got such a potbelly stalking all over the place. This job needed a horse. His team horse was off grazing in hobbles. Riding it bareback, even since it had fattened, would be no great pleasure. He checked the sun time. Must be eight o'clock all ready. He doubled his stride up the ties.

The next day, he sent Brown off to head the rail crew with the new members. He and Ripple reconstructed the payroll. In the shade of a mesquite bush, he learned he made fifty a week as the boss and the leads got fifty cents more a day than the others.

"And I'm giving you a bonus," Ripple said when they had it up to date. "I can see you've already got your part of this operation back in gear. I'm paying you for two weeks as the head man come Saturday night."

"Yes, sir."

"Just remember, if you don't want to be jailed, don't try to come to Lordsburg to spend it." He clapped Slocum on the shoulders. "Don't worry about that. I'll cover for you out here."

"Yes, sir."

They'd celebrate at the ranch when they heard the news of his pay raise. Ramsey might even have the money to buy everything they needed, including the pitcher pump setup.

Things went well for his new job until late Saturday afternoon. Then two wagon loads of whores went shouting and screaming past his crew and headed for the assortment of tents and shelters where the bachelor men lived.

Slocum knew, as horny as most the workers were, it would be hard to keep them concentrating on their work the next few hours.

Some old gal with breasts big as jugs had her dress top off and was waving her tits at them as the wagon went past.

"Here they are, boys! You got a mouth that big? Any of you got a mouth this big?" She hefted them up. Snow white, save for the dark nipple, they looked like white flags to wave at the poor horny men trying to work.

Slocum had had enough. He went past the rail setters and stood with his hands on his hips.

"Get off the railroad property with that flashing or I'll send you packing for good!"

"Don't you want a big titty?" she shouted, flaunting hers at him.

"I want that wagon the hell out of here!" He waved the driver on.

"Hey, you slave driving sumbitch, here's one for you!" One of the whores in the wagon bent over, threw up her dress and mooned him with her big bare ass shining in the sun. The workers all laughed until Slocum's scowl sent them back to work again. At last, the wagons went on to the men's camp.

Three o'clock, they quit early for their pay. The men formed a line outside the new tent with the sides rolled up for air. The Southern Pacific paymaster was guarded by two blue uniformed men armed with shotguns who had arrived with the buckboard and the clerk earlier.

A small rat-faced man without much hair and thick glasses, he checked carefully over Slocum's sheets, then looked up and nodded.

"You're a damn sight better man at bookkeeping than that Irishman that had your job."

"He got killed this week with six others."

"I won't miss him," the little man said with a coldness that even Slocum felt. "I will call the man's name. Him and him alone may come inside the tent, collect this money and then leave. Anyone else comes inside, the guards have orders to blow their brains out. Is that clear?"

"Sure."

"I had one riot where I was making payroll. Won't ever happen again."

Slocum nodded. The little man, who never gave his name, had a heart colder than an iceberg floating down the Platte at Fort Laramie on breakup day. Perhaps he needed to be that tough; he sure wasn't dealing with angels.

"John Allen!" the man called out.

A big man with long, dirt-clogged whiskers stepped inside. The paymaster nodded to the money on the table. Allen removed his filthy hat and dust fell from it. He was bald through the center of his head, the rest a mixture of gray and black curls that hung on the sides in a greasy unwashed mixture.

"Guess I better go get myself bred," Allen said with a chuckle, and money in hand, he nodded to the man. "I like the alphabet way. Gives me firsts on them whores." He flopped on his hat and left with a spring in his walk.

"Apache!" the man called.

The short Indian came inside, went to the table and picked up his money.

"Hey!" The paymaster stopped him. "You any kin to that killer on the loose called Geronimo?"

Apache turned back and grinned. "Him my brother."

Slocum forced himself not to laugh as the paymaster's face turned white. "Get the fuck out of here!"

Unfazed by the words, the Indian strode out like a confident rooster, swaggering as he went. He had shown that haughty little man a thing or two. Ask a stupid question and get a dumber answer. Slocum couldn't wait to tell the others what Apache had told the man.

By four o'clock, everyone had been paid, including Slocum. The iron box was padlocked and the guards were ready to put it on the rig. The paymaster never thanked Slocum.

"See you in two weeks," he said and followed the two guards carrying the trunk out of the tent. Loaded, the little man drove the team, one guard sitting beside him, shotgun ready, the other seated on the strongbox and facing the rear, his scattergun ready too. They headed for Lordsburg.

Already, the shouting whores and the wild men in the tent town had begun a celebration sure to last all night. Men were drinking beer and sloshing it all over each other in their wild melee. A fiddle played, and three females with their arms locked kicked up their legs in French can-can fashion, so some man sitting on his knees could look up under their wagging dresses and see the rest of their butts exposed.

Ramsey and Brown brought Slocum's horse to him.

"Going to be wild here tonight," Ramsey said.

Brown shook his head and wiped his hand over his mouth like a man about to die for drink.

"Lots of sore heads come Monday," Slocum said and leaped up on his horse. Another week they'd have saddles. He'd be ready for one. "You boys ready or want to look longer?"

"Hell, no, if I look any longer, I'll have to go over

there and get in line for some of that pussy," Brown said and reined his horse around.

"I agree," Ramsey said and they rode west. Slocum's only concern was that the drunken men didn't kill too many of each other, so he would have a crew Monday. The wagon loads of whores and liquor, he knew, were the railroad's way to keep the men close to the tracks and broke, so they'd be there for work on Monday. Slocum put heels to his mount and they trotted for home in the hot afternoon. Early for them to get off.

6

"We get this wagon all rigged for him, he can leave at first light," Brown said, going over the best of their harness to use on the four horses that Ramsey would drive to Tucson.

"Yes, if Cyra can get all that money sewed in his vest," Slocum said, looking over to the ramada, where she sat on the new bench they'd made for her and sewed away.

"Sure be glad when we can be ranchers and not railroad laborers."

"Aw, everything has its pitfalls," Slocum said. "But there's less in other things, I agree, than laying track."

The horse deal complete and laid out for the morning, they went over to the shade, where Ramsey cleaned and reloaded the scattergun.

"Keep it handy," Slocum warned.

When the man set it aside, he nodded. "Never had to kill a man in my life."

"I know, but when it gets down to you and him, better it be him than you."

"He's right there, Ram. We're counting on you getting a lot done," Brown said.

"I will."

63

"I know you will, but I mean, we're counting on you getting it done and back here."

The sewing job for her went on, even after supper when the other two had turned in. Cyra sat in the camp firelight and sewed the money in the lining of the vest so it didn't bulge and give it away. Slocum blew on a cup of coffee and watched her.

"We going to that stream you talked about tomorrow?" she asked, looking up at him.

"We can."

She nodded, busy making stitches again. "I can take us along some tortillas and some beans to roll in them."

"Be good. We might see a deer too we can turn into jerky."

Again she looked up at him. "I'd sure like that."

"That old rifle in the wagon shoot?"

"Did the last time my husband used it."

"I'll get it out and clean it. You have some ammo?"

"Yes."

It was a well-used breech-loading Springfield. He couldn't even read the caliber on the rusted barrel, but the bore didn't look too badly corroded. He knew you could nail a tack with some of these older guns. Big enough caliber to bring down a deer, so he busied himself oiling it down.

Satisfied that the weapon was clean, he straddled the bench and looked at her still sewing. She bit off the thread and then turned to him. "Finished."

He nodded. They stared at each other. Some long minutes passed and neither of them moved. Fire in the pit was about out; only a small amount of red light shone on the right side of her face. He scooted down the bench until their faces were only inches apart. She threw her hands around his neck and they kissed.

Then, their mouths apart, she gave a soft sigh. "Been waiting for that."

"Yes," he agreed. "Since the day I looked up and thought you'd thump me with that stick."

"Oh, no."

He hugged her and held her tight. "Till tomorrow?"

"Yes, but what about Brown?" she whispered. "He may want to go along too."

"His turn to guard the place."

"Yes," she said, pleased, and kissed him again.

Ramsey left for Tucson, even before the sun purpled the eastern horizon. Harness jingling, horses fresh and high stepping, he waved at them and headed down the dry wash for the wagon road west.

"Cyra and I want to go see a creek," Slocum said as he squatted on his boot heels with his coffee cup.

"Huh?" Brown asked and frowned at him.

"We want to take one team and the other wagon and go see a real stream today."

Brown finally nodded as if he understood. "We better get it hitched up then."

"I said, Cyra and I—"

"I ain't that dumb—heard you the first time. I want to sleep all day. You two being gone, it ought to be quiet enough to do that. Besides, you two won't be here figuring out chores I need to be a-doing."

"Right." Slocum blew on his coffee. He saw her look up from her cooking and nod in agreement. This would be their day.

Horses hitched and two of them on the seat, they waved goodbye to Brown and left for the Chiricahuas. The clop of the horses' hooves and harness noise set in as the iron wheels rolled along. She scooted over close so their hips bumped together, and then she laughed.

"I don't have much shame."

"Good," he said and gave her look of approval.

"I warned you."

"You warned me." He gave a nod and slapped the horses into a jog with the lines. He wanted to get there.

She tackled his right arm and hugged it. "Been hard the last two weeks. Me not climbing in your bedroll."

"I'd sure have enjoyed it."

"I guess you would have, but I didn't want to face them two in the morning after."

"How long you all been together?"

"Ramsey lost his wife, my husband's sister, before Rand died. Brown and him are kinda half brothers. So Ramsey moved to our place, and Brown came along after that. My husband and I planned to come west. They were coming along. Place we had back there wasn't much. Then he died." She gave a sigh. "Wasn't fair."

She bolted herself up beside him. "He wouldn't want me to spend the rest of my life crying and wringing my hands over him. I sold that old place, and the three of us came on to here."

"Neither of them didn't offer to marry you?" he asked, flicking the right horse for not keeping up.

"They did, and I said, no thanks. I like both of them, but I like them like brothers, not suitors."

"I'm a suitor?"

She rolled her lips inside and then got a sharp look in her eyes. "I know you won't stay, can't—you'll be my suitor for a day, a week. You are the shiny knight who came riding in—"

"With a flour sack over my head and hands tied behind my back?"

"I am not the princess in some castle. You looked good to me." They both laughed.

Middle of the morning, they reached the pungent junipers and he drove up a side canyon. A blue mule deer bolted away and he regretted not having the rifle ready.

As if she understood his thoughts, she drew the long gun out of the back and held it ready for him.

"Next one won't get away," she promised him.

"Right. You have the shells?"

"In my pocket."

The tracks going up the canyon grew rougher. Soon the road ran beside a small silver stream that gurgled over rock and dashed around in the streambed. She nodded her approval as they swayed from side to side on the primitive tracks. With no sign of any recent traffic, he hoped they would have the big hole ahead to themselves.

After a long grade, they pulled into a grove of pines and a grassy meadow. He tied off the reins and turned to her. Their lips met like fiery torches and he hugged her tight as they tasted one another. Until at last they parted for air and he smiled.

"The big swimming hole is under this hill."

"I can't wait," she said and bailed out of the seat after him.

"Could you claim this for a ranch?" she asked.

"Guess so, it isn't Apache land anymore."

"This could be ranch two." Hand in hand they went to look over the edge. Twenty feet beneath them in the streambed nestled a good-sized blue hole of water surrounded by worn rock-faced cliffs and white-trunk sycamores.

"Oh, it's gorgeous!" She clapped her hands together in excitement.

"Let me unharness so the horses can graze and then we can go down there."

"I'll help," she said, and with her skirt in her hand, she rushed over to help undo the animals. Hobbles in place, she carried a blanket and the poke with their lunch. He took along the rifle and wore a feed sack towel around his neck.

"How did you know about this place?"

"Been all over these mountains looking for Apaches."

"With the Army?"

"Yes, with General Crook."

She led the way on the path that descended the mountain. The lower down that they went, the louder the stream sounded in the confines of the cliffs.

"Did you like the Army?"

"It was a job like the railroad. Way to eat."

She stopped and frowned at him. "You have no roots, do you?"

"No."

She shrugged and went on. "Strange, most men look for a nest."

"Something happened a long time ago. I was blamed for it, no way now to erase it. So—I move on."

"I can understand."

Some noisy birds sang in the trees and broke their silence. The murmur of the creek rushing over rocks and spilling out of the damlike structure at the front of the small hole filled the canyon. At last, on a sandy drift beside the water, she spread the blanket. He leaned the rifle against a tree and put the towel on a thick limb growing sideways from the trunk.

"Can we shut our eyes?" she asked. "And undress."

"You ashamed?"

"No, but I feel so . . . uncomfortable undressing before you."

"I will turn and allow you to undress."

"Thanks," she said, pleased, and began to undo the small buttons down the front of her dress.

He took a seat on the blanket with his back to her and eased off his run-over boots. The tight muscles in his back complained as he fought the last one off. At last free, he held the boot and watched a small bird bathe itself at the edge. Her movements behind him drew a smile on his face when he set the boot down.

"Is the water cold?"

"Usually cool," he said and unbuttoned his shirt.

"You look away and I'll try it."

"Sure," he said, with his back to her, and took off his shirt. He rose to his knees and unbuttoned his pants.

"Aeee!" she cried and he turned.

Her elbows tight to her sides and her hands covering her breasts, she stood knee deep in the water. Her eye squeezed shut, she cried out, "It's ice cold!"

"Naw," he said and shucked his pants off. In two long strides, he reached the edge and dove out in the water. He swam across the hole. Standing up to his knees in the pool, he swept the hair back from his face and grinned at her.

Neck-deep and dog paddling, she made faces at him. "It's cold."

"Not bad after all the heat I've been in." He dove in again and swam over to her.

Their eyes met and they both stood. Water streaming off them, he stepped to her and felt her arms in his grasp as he raised her up. Their faces met in a kiss and he swept her up in his arms, carrying her as she cradled his face between her hands and kissed him with the sweetness of a dew on a rose.

He placed her on the blanket and sprawled beside her. Their wet skin together caused friction. The sparks of it soon had them so intoxicated that when he moved on top, her legs parted and he slipped between them. He nosed his rising shaft into her gates and she sighed—"Yes."

All the emotions pent up in both of them began to fester. She raised her butt up off the blanket to meet him, and soon his shaft was buried deep in her nest. They sought relief; they sought completion. His rock-hard butt drove his dick homeward. Her muscle-hard stomach met his thrusts, and their pelvic bones ground their pubic hair between them.

Until at last the head of his dick stretched to proportions beyond belief. He felt the shot of his cannon begin the trip out the gun barrel. The cheeks of his ass cramped and he plunged forward; the explosion made him faint.

Her eyes closed in pleasure as they fell into a heap.

"Never . . . never . . . ," she mumbled, clutching him to her. "It never felt that good in my life. Am I wanton?"

"No," he assured her, raising up on his elbow. "We awoke something is all."

"Awoke, oh—" She put her hand to her forehead and shook her head. "I knew I wanted you, but . . . I cautioned myself . . ."

"For what?" he asked, looking at her fine pear-shaped breasts, the light brown stain of her small nipples topping them. He wanted to taste them, kiss them and feel their weight.

"That I was evil wanting you and it wouldn't be—oh, like this." She swooned, then threw her arms out wide. Over their heads, some raucous ravens scolded them from the treetops.

He cupped her breast, looked intently into her green eyes for a sign of any protest and, seeing none, dropped his mouth to taste it.

"Oh!" she cried in a wavering voice and clutched him to her. "My God, my God, I love it. Don't ever stop."

7

"I'm trying not to look drunk," she said as the wagon and team started up the last mile for the ranch. "I know Brown will know—"

"Not much we can do about it," he said, puzzled about how to hide her obvious euphoria.

"Been around them too long. I can't hide much."

"Well, damn, I'm sorry if I'm going to cause you any grief."

She frowned at him and then shook her head. "Grief? No grief. My lands, I didn't feel this wonderful on my honeymoon." Then she paused and shook her head in disapproval. "That sounds bad."

"Maybe you were entitled to have a good time after all you've been through."

"That doesn't sound good either."

"Hey, out here, you have to lead your own life. Who do you answer to? Your own self. Don't try to please someone snooty or someone you don't even know. Out here, you better live every day to the fullest," he said and slapped the horses to make them trot.

"You're right. If I act love-drunk, they'll have to put up with it. I love them, but I still have my own to live."

"That's better," Slocum said and slapped the team again on the butt. It would soon be sundown; Brown would think they had gone off forever.

A short time later, he drove the team up the bank. He turned them back toward the house, and she let out a stifled cry.

"What's wrong with Coffee?"

Brown was slumped down with his hands tied spread-eagle to the new hitch, and his bare head hung limp. Slocum hauled in the horses, set the brake and twisted off the reins, all the time looking hard at the form on the rack.

He put his hand on her leg. "Stay here. I'll go see about him. Get the rifle out. Whoever done this may still be around here."

"I will. Think he's alive?"

He shook his head without any idea. He crossed to where Brown hung. On his knees, he spoke to the man.

"You alive?"

"That you, Slocum?" he whispered.

"Who did this?"

"They jumped me. Right . . . after you two left."

Slocum was on his feet undoing the ropes. "He's alive. Get him some water."

She agreed and rushed off for the clay ollyah. Returning with it and a dipper gourd, she helped sprawl the man over Slocum's lap.

He slurped the water, then choked and coughed up some.

"Easy, easy." Slocum shared a hard look with her and turned back. "Who did this?"

"Two white guys—said they were looking for you."

"What did you tell them?" she asked.

"Nothing. They tied me to that hitching rack and used their fists on me. Told 'em nothing."

"You didn't need to take that beating for me."

"Yeah, I sure did, 'cause she was with you."

"Coffee Brown—" She shook her head at him and stopped. "Did he die?"

"No, passed out. He sure took a heckuva beating." Slocum looked around. He owed those two bastards for this too, besides Rosa's death.

"Let's get him in my bed," she said, raising up. "Do you know who would do this?"

"A couple of bounty hunters. Called Radamacher and Delaware."

"Why—"

"Coffee's lucky to even be alive. They killed my friend in Mexico."

She put her hands to her face. "Oh, no."

He carried Brown by his arms, she by his feet, to her bed inside the jacal. They took off his shoes, undressed him and soon had him under the sheet. He moaned a few times, blinked at them and passed out again. She sat on the side of the bed and put cool compresses on his battered face.

Slocum excused himself and went around in the last of the sunset to check for their tracks. Two horses—he tried to recall the hoofprints of the ponies they rode. He would know them if he saw them again.

Ramsey gone to Tucson, Brown in tough shape and her to be left alone out there while he worked—it didn't make things set any too well with him. Someone from the track crew who went to Lordsburg must have got too loose talking the night before and those two found out and headed up here to find him. What could he do about them? One worn-out Springfield rifle and a handful of shells wasn't much artillery against those two. Hardly better than a slingshot.

"He's doing better," she said in the candlelight. With a wrung-out cloth in her hand, she went back to the bedside.

"Good. Keep that rifle close. You know how to use it?"

"Yes—but."

"Your life and Coffee's may depend on you shooting someone, if necessary. These guys don't play games."

She swallowed hard. "What are you going to do?"

"Try to stop them."

"How? You have no pistol, nothing?"

He blew out the candle. "I have darkness and an Apache who will hate this."

"What—an Apache?"

"Be calm. I'll be back in a few hours. They aren't liable to return here. If they do, shoot them and ask questions later." He hugged her trembling shoulder. "Take care of him and don't build a fire."

"In the dark?"

"Yes. You can find your way around without the candle and don't make a big fire. Best not to make one at all."

"I won't, but I'm worried about you."

"Don't be. I'll return in a few hours."

"Be careful." She jumped up and hugged him. "Oh, please be careful."

He found Apache's wickiup in the starlight. The Indian answered from inside when Slocum hooted at him like an owl. In an instant, he came outside and squatted on the ground beside Slocum.

"What's wrong?"

"Two bounty hunters came to my place and tortured Brown. One is short and bug-eyed, the other taller and bearded."

"I saw them. They have a camp west of here." He nodded slow-like, considering what he should do about them. Apache didn't miss that much that went on—lucky for him.

"I want rid of them."

The squatted Indian made the sign of "knife" with the side of his hand passing over his throat.

"No . . . That would bring the law down here, and I'd have to leave. I want these two to stew and wonder."

"Scare them?"

"Yes, but how?" Slocum had no answers.

"Put plenty of cactus pads in boots and saddle blankets. Make sign with arrows?"

"Yeah, I want them to worry and fret, plus get the hell out of here."

"Good, we do."

Slocum nodded, satisfied that the plan was what he wanted.

An hour later, he squatted next to the Indian in the moonlight. Apache nodded and they stole in closer to the quiet camp. Slocum dragged the prickly pear cactus segments between two sticks. Apache held up his hand and indicated for him to stay there. Then, like a shadow, Apache took the cactus and worked his way in closer.

The starlight shone off Apache's knife blade as he deftly sliced the pads. He put pieces of spiny cactus in each of the four boots, then a few pads were placed between their double horse blankets. He left the others scattered on the ground so they would be stepped on by the unaware. In the middle of the camp, he stuck two arrows in the ground to make an X. Then without a sound he came back to where Slocum squatted.

Using a handful of greasewood branches, Apache swept their tracks away.

"This will make them know Apaches have been there," he said, and they worked their way back to their horses.

Just so long as it scared those two off. Most men who lived in the Southwest did not like to believe that "ghost people" had visited their camp during the night—undetected—and left such unwanted presents as the prickly pear, instead of killing them, which is what the "ghosts" could have easily done. It should make the two clear out and in a hurry. Slocum had to hope this worked until he had a better remedy for that pair of killers.

Under the stars, he and Apache parted with a wave at a trail fork, and he rode the big horse for home. There would be precious few hours left for him to sleep. If this only worked—that concerned him more than sleep.

"You need to talk to Coffee," she said, pouring Slocum a cup in the predawn darkness. "He insists that he's going to work today. He's in no condition."

"He's the one has to work." Slocum shrugged. "We can let him try it. I see he's in trouble, I can pull him off."

She shook her head in disapproval and in a swish of her dress tail went off to the ramada.

"Go ahead," she said sharply. "Kill yourself. Haven't a lick more sense than that."

"I'll be all right," Brown complained.

"Sure and die out there."

He came and joined Slocum. "She's on a tear."

Staring after her, he nodded, thinking more about the willowy figure under the dress than what his partner had said. Whew, he was ready to go back to the Blue Hole. Instead, he must face the track crew and another hot dusty day. The coffee burned his tongue when in his absence of mind he sipped it before it cooled. The discovery brought a smile to his sun-cracked lips; served him right, thinking about her sensuous body when he should be on other things.

He left her strict instructions: shoot to kill. With a nod, she indicated the loaded rifle leaning against the dry sink under the ramada.

"I will be ready."

He nodded and booted his horse after Brown's.

"Will they be back?" Brown asked as they descended the steep slope.

"I hope not," Slocum said, looking up at the filthy straw brim of the old hat she had given him to wear weeks earlier. How long would his disguise work? Obviously they had looked for him and had not been satisfied of his identity, clean-shaven and his hair short. Still they were no fools and wanted the reward; by this time were probably desperate.

Apache did not show up for work. Slocum wondered about his absence, but several more men were missing. Typical of a Monday morning after payday. The next thing all those men who had contracted the clap from the whores would begin to fall out. Being track-laying boss on Monday morning was not the best job to have, he decided.

To begin, he put a rail-and-tie crew together by using some of the men from the teamsters to fill in. Not a popular situation, but Slocum needed to show Ripple he could lay tracks under the worst conditions.

He saw two men coming from the west, riding a familiar horse double. It was the two bounty hunters and Radamacher was even hatless. They went past on their trotting horse and never noticed him, Radamacher looked uncomfortable on the back of Del's saddle. Too bad, Slocum decided. They acted like they were leaving the country.

Apache appeared shortly and walked up to Slocum. "One horse threw the short one. Then he run off. They can't walk far." He laughed to himself. "Too many needles in their boots."

"Good. Get on the rail crew and send that teamster Farley back to his mules." Slocum looked off in the direction that the bounty hunter pair had gone. Perhaps Cyra would be safe. He hoped so.

With a quick nod, Apache moved off to obey.

Nine A.M., Ripple came with the work train and brought all the men he had bailed out of the Lordsburg jail. They moaned and groaned, and after a while Slocum had his crew straightened again and was discussing things with his boss.

"How many men are you short?"

"One teamster's missing. Ramsey had to go to Tucson on business. But I think, on the construction crew, I must be three short."

Ripply nodded. "Two men were shot over the weekend in barroom brawls. Well, one was shot and the other knifed, and one guy who worked for you is in jail over that. That's probably the rest."

"Are there more workers in Lordsburg?"

"I'll find you some. I am amazed that you could even start laying track this morning."

"Worked fine. Teamsters don't like to haul rail or set ties, but they can when I'm short men." Slocum considered the distant Chiricahuas. "If I should have to leave here unexpected, pay my wages to Coffee Brown."

Ripple blinked at him. "You leaving—"

"May have to. But not yet."

"You tell me who's bugging you, I'll throw them in the slammer."

"There may be too many to do that."

"Mob, you mean?"

Slocum shook his head. "Some old scars may fester."

"Damn, I hope not soon. Now, that grade to the west—"

Slocum listened to the man ramble on about the plans for the track ahead. If Radamacher and Delaware had got that close to him—how far away were the Abbott brothers? A little game of prickly pear and a few arrows wasn't going to scare the likes of them four for long. Ramsey better hurry back—he'd sure need that pistol. He considered asking Ripple for one—perhaps he had a spare.

"I was wondering," Slocum began when they finished the railroad business. "You don't have a spare revolver, do you?"

Ripple paused, pursed his lips together and then nodded. "Yes, have a small one in my saddlebags. My lands, you sure need one dealing with all these thugs and outlaws."

"I'll return it."

"No problem." He drew out a small five-shot .22 called a Ladysmith. He shook his head handing it over. Then he drew out a drawstring cloth sack of cartridges. "Not an arsenal, but it is firepower."

Slocum nodded, checking over the well-oiled pistol. "What do I owe you?"

"Nothing, but I sure hope you don't need to use it."

Slocum agreed and slipped the handgun in his hip pocket. It would be perfect for her protection. He could show her how to use it and feel much better. Ramsey needed to hurry back.

Noontime, he checked on Brown's condition, but the man waved away his concern.

"You see them two ride by this morning?" Slocum asked under his breath.

"Yeah, I wondered about that."

"They had pancakes for breakfast," Slocum said with a grin.

"Pancakes?"

"Yeah, pancake cactus in their boots and saddle blankets."

Brown snickered. "That serves them right."

Slocum agreed, grateful they hadn't killed the poor man. He'd never be certain why they hadn't, cold-blooded as they'd been with Rosa. Perhaps they thought they'd get away with murder down there in Mexico. Prickly pear wasn't enough punishment for those two. But their dead bodies would have needed to be explained, and would have also brought more law there. He'd done the right thing with Apache. Besides, the damn Injun liked it.

•   •   •

Late in the week, Ramsey was back in camp when Slocum and Brown returned from work in late afternoon. He was leaned against a ramada post whittling on a stick when they dropped from their horses.

"How did it go?" Brown asked, out of breath.

"Not bad. We have a brand. It's a Three Bar C." He picked up a new iron by the handle and showed them the design on the end. Cyra looked up from her cooking and shared a pleased wink with Slocum as they huddled around Ramsey.

"The place?" Brown asked.

"It's registered in her name."

"Great! The goods?"

"Come over here," Ramsey said and led them to the well. The new red pitcher pump sat on top of the frame he'd made with fresh lumber over the hole. "Well, work it."

Brown took hold of the handle and began to slosh water in the foot tub under it. "Here, Slocum, you pump. I want to soak my head."

"I got each of us a usable saddle, a cap-and-ball pistol and plenty of rope."

"And baking powder," Cyra announced and held out some browned biscuits on a tin plate. "Be careful, they're hot."

"When we going cowboying?" Brown asked, tossing the too-hot bread from hand to hand.

After supper, they lounged around the ramada seated on the ground. Slocum felt dressed with the pistol strapped on in a well-worn cross-draw holster. Never mind, at least he was armed. Looking across at her, he felt better. She had Ripple's little pistol and knew how to shoot it if necessary.

"I say we should work for the railroad until they get so far west we can't ride back here at night," Slocum explained. "Their money's good and you will need it. Cow business is slow pay."

"Makes sense," Ramsey said. "I don't relish it, but we can make good money and we'll need it."

"I was just wanting to quit that business, but I agree the money will help us later. What's Tucson like?" Brown asked.

"Dusty, hot. Narrow streets, mostly Messikins—ain't a real pretty place." Ramsey shook his head.

Brown shrugged as if disappointed. "Don't sound too great."

Slocum nodded. Ramsey was right—Tucson, for the center of things in southern Arizona, was not the prettiest place and it was Spanish. He could recall a dark-eyed dancer clacking her way across a hard-packed cantina floor toward him, trumpets and fiddles making the fast step music. Hands above her head, she twisted around and around to the song like some kind of vine.

Hours later, after the cantina closed, she still had the same muscular fury in her body lying underneath him in her narrow cot. Her back arched to meet his thrusts and she cried out loud for him to give her more and more. He was wondering if he could stand any more, when at last he drove his final inches into her and reached the bottom. Something deep inside her coupled with the strained head of his dick and he came. Then the hot rush of her come flushed out of her and rushed over his scrotum as she held him tight inside, until she melted into a small pile under him. What was her name? He could not recall.

8

Slocum never looked directly at them until their backs were turned and they were past him—four riders headed for the tent camp of the workers. The most obvious thing in the too bright sun was the blanket-rump Appaloosa that Ferd Abbott rode. He recognized the other three as well. Lyle Abbott was the fourth horseman.

He found Brown overseeing the rail crew. When they set down the iron beam in place, he called him aside.

"Trouble arrived a few minutes ago. No, don't look. You tell Ripple I said I was sorry—listen to me."

"I am. You going to leave?" Brown blinked his eyes as if confused by the whole matter.

"Have to. You give Ripple my day sheets. I already told him to pay you my remaining wages." He handed the small ledger to him.

"But . . . what will you do?"

"I better not tell you. Then you won't have to tell them."

"I wouldn't tell nobody nothing."

"I know that, don't get upset. You can't help my deal. I've stayed too long."

"Who's going to be the boss?" Brown looked around puzzled.

"I'll send Ramsey back to do that."

Looking more confident, Brown agreed. "He can handle it."

"I know. See you."

"Damn—"

"Hush."

Brown nodded and shook his head. Slocum set out going down the fill on the north side, where he was out of sight, and headed for the teamsters. The fill would conceal him until he found Ramsey.

"You're the new boss," Slocum told him. "Get up there and keep things going."

Mopping his sweaty face on his kerchief, Ramsey paused and blinked at him. "How come?"

"Haven't got that much time. Maybe someday you will understand."

Ramsey stared hard at the fill as if full of questions. "That means I'm the boss, huh?"

"Right, get to work."

He stuck out his hand and they shook. "Been a pleasure. May break her heart."

He ignored the man's words. Leaving her was the real hard part. "I'm taking the horse. I won't go by there. You'll have to tell her—she didn't want me to."

"Damn, Slocum, you made me the boss and tell her too—you ain't easy."

"Life don't come that way."

"Here, take twenty dollars. Take it. You'll need something."

"Thanks." With that said, Slocum shoved the money in his pocket and hurried for the hobbled horses, where he tossed his saddle on the big bay and cinched him down. Looking back to wave at Ramsey, he booted the bay into a trot headed north.

•   •   •

Two days later, Slocum met a drover and two Mexicans
with a hundred head of steers. The man was white, though
he wore a high peaked hat and poncho and rode a Mexican saddle. His bushy mustache was white on top but
brown stained from tobacco around his mouth.

"Where you headed?" Slocum asked, looking over the
herd of steers grazing in the late afternoon.

"Fort McDowell. You ever been there?"

"Time or two."

"Got an army contract to deliver these beeves there."

Slocum nodded at him. "You reckon it's any good?"

The man's blue eyes blinked and he spluttered, "What . . .
what the hell do you mean?"

"I mean they been selling phony contracts and when
the seller gets there, he's stuck."

"You ever seen a phony one?" The man's silver-blue
eyes widened.

"No, but I've seen a good one."

The man dug the papers out of his saddlebags and
handed them over.

With a quick check, Slocum went over the contract,
then read the signature. It looked official enough, so he
nodded in approval.

"You seem to know a lot about this business."

"I've been around these agency sales. There's lots of
underhanded dealing and things like phony contracts going around."

"Name's Nelson."

"Slocum."

"You riding through? I could use a good hand who
knows the way."

"I've got the time. Once we cross the Gila, there isn't
any water for three days unless it rains."

"These old longhorns'll make that."

"I figured so."

"Step down, Slocum, and light yourself on the ground. We'll have some frijoles cooked here in a little while. You coming out of the south?" Nelson tossed his head in that direction.

"Mexico. Decided I needed some cooler air."

"Yeah boy, it's hot around here."

"It will be hot like this until fall unless you get up in the high country."

"You mean like Preskitt?"

"Yeah," Slocum agreed. The man must be familiar with the territorial capitol because he called it by its real name, not Prescott.

"I may have to go there next," Nelson said and wiped his face on his shirtsleeve.

Slocum watched a buzzard circle on the thermals. He glanced back to the south and the heat waves distorted the saw-edge mountains. Had he shed himself of the bounty hunters? He hoped that he had and that they left his friends alone—especially her.

The Mexicans' names were Robles and Chico. Both hardly out of their teens, they were obviously accustomed to this work. The smaller one cooked the beans, and the other one repaired the pack saddle girth and nodded to him.

"Where are you from?" Slocum asked the older man.

"Texas. I drove some cattle to Fort Bowie last year. I decided to stick around these parts and bought up these steers in Sonora, trailed them north and finally got a sale for them."

"You have much trouble in Mexico?"

"Some, but these are good boys." Nelson tossed his head at the twosome. "We managed to avoid the bandits. More of them were white than Messikin."

"You're lucky," Slocum said, thinking that the man was tough too, besides lucky, to have survived. For one man with the long tooth and two unarmed boys to manage to bring a herd out of Mexico unscathed, even a small one, was more than a miracle.

The older man shook his head to dismiss his concern. "I wasn't born yesterday either."

"I savvy, You'll reach the Gila tomorrow. Better rest the cattle a day or so around there, because it is a hard drive on to the Salt from there. At least three days without water."

"We can do that."

Slocum used his horse blanket to sleep on and awoke early from the desert's predawn chill. Cold without a cover, he got up and built up the fire. Soon Robles joined him.

"You forgot your bedroll?" he asked in Spanish.

"*Sí*, I left too quick."

The boy grinned and stirred the pot of leftover frijoles. That would be their breakfast, Slocum assumed. Better than what he had eaten the past two days: a few handfuls of hohoba beans and some unripe prickly pear fruit. Intentionally he had tried to avoid contact with anyone so his pursuers couldn't trace him.

The four ate in silence. No coffee—they had some slick tepid water from a small wooden barrel for drinking. Then Slocum saddled the bay with the others and they gathered the steers, who were docile enough that they moved like oxen.

Nelson sat aboard his horse on a rise and counted the steers until he was satisfied they were all there. Then he nodded and the drive began. Their hooves churning up the pale dust, the cattle followed the lead steer's bell. Slocum rode to the right side, but the steers showed no signs of doing anything but moving in their established pattern.

"They're trail broke," Nelson said and rode his bull-necked blue roan up beside him. The horse had once been a stud, long headed and sloped rump; he resembled the crosses between mustangs and draft animals that cropped up.

"Old Monty ain't purty, but he's a tough bastard," Nelson said.

"Looks that way," Slocum said to make talk.

Nelson spat and wiped his mustache on the back of his hand. "Looks ain't everything. Best piece of ass I ever had in my life was from the ugliest woman in south Texas." Then he laughed aloud and spit off into the greasewood brush again. "So you can't always tell about looks."

Slocum agreed. The sun was beginning to heat up; the long chain of steers marched northward. By late afternoon, he could see some green ahead.

"Them's the cottonwoods along the Gila."

The older man raised up in the stirrups, squinted and then nodded. "We'll rest there. What's your business in this damn desert?"

"Been working on those new railroad tracks."

"Whew, that was work."

"Paid good."

"I reckon so."

"You going to gather another herd after this one?" Slocum asked.

"I'd have to bribe someone in that Tucson Ring to sell a bigger herd. Lucky I made this deal."

"You have to bribe someone?"

"No, not this time. No one wanted to mess with this small a drive. But if I hadn't bought these cattle cheap in Mexico, I wouldn't make any money on them."

Slocum twisted and studied the land. A few tall saguaros grew on the ridges feeding into the flats. The rest was covered with scrub brush and sun-cured tufts of brown grass about belly high. No dust to indicate any pursuit; perhaps he had lost them.

"You looking for work?"

Slocum nodded. "In a cooler place."

They both laughed. Nelson offered him his canteen. Slocum shook his head. In another hour, they'd be at the Gila, and the river wouldn't be half as bad as the water they'd drank out of the barrel.

"It won't be cooler, but I know two good men and a woman have a good claim. They also have a brand."

"They have any cattle?"

"Not yet, but they have a registered brand. I'd bet there's plenty of wild ones up and down the San Pedro and that range east for the four of you to gather."

"What did you say their name was?"

Slocum grinned and told him their names.

"I might drift down there."

"You can use my name."

Nelson spit aside, then righted himself in the saddle. "I may do that. Lots of wild cattle in the brush?"

"I saw plenty."

"Be like the old days in south Texas. They were there for the taking with a long rope and an iron. You ever been to Abilene?"

Slocum nodded.

"Froze my ass off up there in Kansas one winter. The price fell and I had to either carry them over or eat them."

"Makes you think this heat ain't half-bad," Slocum said.

"You're right. Bet we know some of the same folks."

"Probably. Them steers can smell that water."

"Let them go!" he shouted to the boys in Spanish and waved them off. "It'll be *bueno*." He turned back to Slocum. "Been a big herd, they'd pile up, but this bunch ain't going to hurt themselves.

"You know, Slocum, I ain't talked to a white man over ten words in two years. Plumb nice to have you along."

The steers soon filled with water, then they lay down beside the flowing brown stream. Contented, they began to chew their cuds and slap their ears at flies. Slocum rode upstream and bellied down for a good drink. Beside him, the bay horse raised his head and let the water drip from his mouth before he went back for more.

The bridle hung on the horn, Slocum let the horse graze. He'd unsaddle him later. The other three had picked a shady spot under a rattling cottonwood, the leaves rustling in the hot wind. Slocum caught the horse by the mane and took him over there to drop his saddle off and hobble him.

"That pony's been in harness some time," Nelson said, lying on his side and propped up on his arm.

"Last Sunday," Slocum said. "He ain't half-bad either."

"You're full of things that's diffcrent," Nelson said. "Riding a work horse, drifting. Quit a good job."

"Good *paying*," Slocum said and stretched out on his back on the ground. He was trying to forget her—leaving without a word. She was the one asked for it that way. "Not a good job."

"Never built no railroad tracks."

"Don't. It's hard work. Why leave Texas?" Slocum studied the spinning round-shaped leaves above them. Even the hot wind felt good; later he planned to bathe.

"Feud. Damn feud. My family and another family named Raths got into it over a hog. It had my father's earmark on it—or it once had it and someone cut that ear off and the Raths put their mark on the other side.

"Words led to guns. Elbert Raths died that day. My pappy's face was bleeding and I figured he would die. That was a scratch from a bullet was all. But guns drawn, we backed away from each other. My ma standing in the wagon, her screaming, 'If my man dies, I'll kill all you white trash!' Her a-standing there with a shotgun cocked and ready to use it."

Nelson spit. "Pa lived. They shot my oldest brother in the back coming home from a dance the next week. But a week later, my uncle Donovan evened that in a little bar-store down at Dead Water. He gunned down two of them Raths brothers. War was on.

"Caught my pa by himself, making cedar stakes, and killed him with an ax." Nelson looked off at the distant hazy mountains. "Then they gunned down my mother and burned us out.

"I came home to that one day to find what was left. Been on a trail drive to Kansas. Wind had scattered the ashes. They'd put a small cross up over her grave—you know you can kill and kill and never feel no better?"

Slocum agreed with a soft "Yes." He knew that too.

9

The second day after leaving the Gila, they drove the cattle around the base of Superstition Mountain. The great desert basin spread to the west, and Slocum recalled that somewhere down there at Lehi and Mesa, the Mormons had irrigated farm settlements. And some white men had large hay meadows west of the Mormons that they also watered out of the Salt and made a fortune selling their forage to the Army.

In the north, a small red butte soon stuck up, and Slocum knew from past experiences that was close to the Army outpost of Fort McDowell. Without a break, except at night, they'd pushed the longhorn steers hard. Both horses and men were near exhaustion under the double-hot sun and boiling dust. But at last in the late afternoon, they reached an escarpment and the Salt River shone beneath them in the dazzling sun. Steers began to give coarse bawls taking the trail headed for the bottoms and the long awaited drink. The four riders reined up and let their horses breathe.

"You did good, Slocum. I was about to give up getting here."

"Let them rest awhile here and they should have good weight back on them in three or four days."

"What do I owe you?"

"Nothing. You can cross the Salt here and then back across the Verde to the fort and agency. Won't be as deep as after the two rivers flow together west of here. But it probably won't matter unless they have a big rain back up in the mountains."

"I could pay you something."

"No, I'll head on. You fed me."

"Slocum, if I go find them people of yours?" Nelson scrubbed the beard stubble on his cheek as if deeply considering it.

"Tell them I sent you." Slocum met the man's sharp look, nodded and headed his horse westward.

Nelson acted satisfied his name was permission enough. A few miles west, Slocum found a way off the cliffs and rode across the bottom to the river. It rushed past him over rock and ripples, a lot clearer stream than the Gila. After a quick drink, he washed his face and remounted. It was after dark when he reached Lehi.

A light was on in the main store, and Slocum reined up before it. Not much at this crossroads settlement—a few frame and adobe houses in addition to Yarbourough's, the store, with warehouses behind. Across the road were some corrals and the ward, as the Mormons called their church.

Slocum dropped wearily to the ground, gained his sea legs then hitched his horse to the rack. A can or two of tomatoes might quench his thirst. The notion made his teeth float in the back of his mouth. He climbed the stairs and entered the front door. An older man looked up from his books under a lamp.

Black bearded, stern faced, he looked the picture of someone interrupted and not pleased by it.

"Who are you?" he asked gruffly, putting his pen down.

"A man passing through," Slocum said, feeling a little put out at the man's attitude. It wasn't polite to demand from strangers who they were.

"Well, we don't cotton to drifters in Lehi."

"Guess you do sell canned tomatoes—even to drifters."

The man folded his arms over his white shirt. Then he shook his head. "Don't even want to do business with your kind."

Slocum looked at the tin-squared ceiling for help, then he glared at the man. "Those lamps were on, that door was open and this is a business, right?"

"Not for your kind."

"Who owns this place?"

"I do."

"Yarborough, huh?"

"You better clear out of here before I call the law."

"Holler big and loud. I want two cans of tomatoes. How much?" That call-the-law business was a bluff; Slocum knew it.

"Two dollars."

"Two dollars? I suppose you rob everyone like that— being as you're the only store in town."

"That's my price to drifters!"

"Well, Mr Yarborugh, you can stuff them cans up your butt."

"Hmm," he snorted.

"Keep them hands in sight or you might get blowed away." Slocum started for the doorway, so filled with disgust he knew he better ride on before he did something worse.

"And don't come back!"

In the doorway, Slocum nodded. "Thanks for the nice welcome to Lehi." He touched his hat and went to his horse. For a long moment he considered the man in the lighted doorway, then he made two tries at mounting and in the end rode off.

He felt sorry for his old partner Jim Branch, who had to deal with a man like Yarborough. Wonder Jim hadn't got into it with the old man. Knowing Jim, he probably had—Slocum reined the horse around and headed for

Jim's place. Be good to see him and Ruby again. They should have a passel of kids by this time.

That Yarborough needed a good lesson—maybe he'd give him one before he left the valley.

He reined the tired horse in the dark driveway, and a chorus of dogs came to bark at him.

"Who's out there?" a woman's voice called out.

"This Jim Branch's place?"

"No." The woman made a face trying to make him out in the light of the lamp held high in her hand.

"Ruby?"

"Yes. Who're you?"

"Slocum," he said, in hardly more than a whisper. Head down, his weary horse snorted in the dust, and the dogs whined circling around him.

She blew out the lamp and hurried off the porch. "My god. It is you," she gushed and threw her arms around him. A tall, ample-bodied woman, her hug smothered him and her lips closed on his whisker-bristled mouth.

"I'm dirty as a hog," he apologized.

"That's no mind." She kissed him again, this time sticking her hot tongue in his mouth, and he clutched her queenly body to his.

Then she stepped back, giving a wary glance at the house. "My children—I better see to them or they'll be asking all kinds of questions. Put your horse in the corral—can you stay awhile?"

"Awhile—where's Jim?"

She wet her lips in the light coming from the open front door. "You didn't hear? He drowned six months ago."

"Oh, I'm sorry . . ."

"No need. You're here now." Then she turned and in a tone of impatience spoke to the small faces in the doorway. "It's a friend of your father's. Get back to bed."

"Aw—"

"I'll get some water heating. You do sure need a bath."
She turned around again and frowned at the small, curious
faces in the doorway. "I'll cut me a switch in just a minute
if all of you aren't in bed."

"Sure, I'm not . . ." He looked pained toward the house.
Was his being there an inconvenience or an imposition on
her?

"Not what?" She threw her head back and laughed. The
wonderful reddish chestnut curls that framed her face
shook with her mirth. "You don't know—oh, we'll have
time to talk later. I said, get to bed!" She stalked up the
stairs waving a threatening finger that sent the pitter-pat
of little feet fleeing.

Slocum turned the bay loose in the corral with a couple of
draft horses. There he had plenty of hay and water. Slocum
watched him, under the starlight, drop to his front knees and
roll over on his back several times, grunting at the effort.

She looked for him from the back doorway. Her ample
figure was silhouetted against the house light. When he
stepped on the porch, she smiled. "They're in bed, but
sure not asleep, so we need to keep our voices down."

"Sure. What happened to Jim?"

"We had a flood on the Salt last winter. Our—The community's dam upstream looked to be in danger from the
flooding, so the men were up there fortifying it. Jim fell
in and was swept away. Took three days to find his body."

"Sorry to hear that."

"Nothing anyone could have done. Flood got the dam
anyway."

"How are you making it?" he whispered.

"Making it. Except Bishop Fletcher wants me to marry
some old man."

"So . . ."

"So I'm not marrying some old man that I'll have to
care for the rest of his life. I'll marry me a real husband
or do without." Her eyes glinted with fury.

"How is the farm?"

"Fine. I can hire a little help and I'll get it all done. Jim had this place in good shape when I lost him." She looked him over inspectively. "Water's getting hot. I had some heating on the stove before you came."

"Good."

She stood up and blew out the lamp. "Get undressed then."

Slocum smiled, and in the shadowy starlight coming in the windows, he could see her pouring water in a bathtub. He removed his shirt, holster, toed off his worn out boots, then dropped his pants. Socks and underwear came off next. He stepped around the table and the dogs began to bark in the yard.

"Now, who would that be?" she said. "Get in. I'll go see and send them on their way."

"Ma! Ma! Someone else's coming!" a small voice called from the loft over the kitchen.

"I hear one more peep, I am beating bottoms. Hear me?" she said, and headed for the front door.

"Yes."

Just in case, Slocum set his pistol on top of a chair close by. Where he was at, he couldn't see the front door, but he knew she had gone outside on the porch.

"Sister Branch?"

"Yes?"

"Sister Branch, it's Brother Cox."

"For heaven's sake, what are you doing here at this hour of the night?"

"Thought you might be lonely, Sister."

"No, I'm not lonely. My Jim hasn't been in the ground that long, Brother Cox."

"I didn't mean lonely like that— I meant lonely for . . . you know what I mean?"

"Brother Cox, I am not lonely for anything. You get along now. My children are trying to go to sleep."

"Very well. You're a lovely lady, Sister Branch. I sure didn't want you to suffer none."

"I'll be fine."

"See you at church Sunday."

"Yes, good night."

Slocum used the rag he found on the side of the tub. The warm water intoxicated him as the steam vapors ran up his nose. He rubbed away at the layers of dirt and looked up when he heard her finally return.

"The nerve of him," she huffed.

"That the man the bishop picked out for you?"

"No, that one's married and fifty years old. Lonely? I'll lonely him."

She dropped to her knees and took the rag away from him. "Here, I have the soap."

"Good. That can get another layer off."

"Where've you been?" she hissed.

"Working on the railroad down near the New Mexico border."

"Why— I mean, I'm glad to see you, really glad, but why did you come by here?"

"I needed a place to lay low. Got some bounty hunters on my tracks down there. But I left them nothing to follow."

Her hand on the cloth, she rubbed over the corded muscles of his stomach, going lower and lower with each pass. Then she let out an audible exhale with "My god, that's one nice brace and bit."

She sought his lips with her mouth and the snaking tongue soon mixed with his. Her efforts to unroot him at the same time only added to his erection and soon they were standing, kissing. Water cascading off him, her dress front was soon soaked, but that did not slow their hunger for each other. She quickly unbuttoned her dress and stripped it off. Their naked bodies meshed together.

"Where?" he asked in her ear as both of them tried to regain their breath.

"Floor," she managed and started getting down.

In a flash, she was on her back, pulling him on top of her. He found her slot and began to drive his nail home. Her full legs raised, and his butt drove him home with a sigh of pleasure from her lips. She held her legs up beside him and rocked him as furiously as he drove into her.

Savoring every moment, he wished for a bed. The floor must be killing her back, he worried, but the stiffness in his dick felt no compassion, nor did the aching in his butt to stuff her full each time. Then his speed increased and she clutched him tight. The end came as an explosion, and she wilted as he gave her his all.

"Thank God, at last, my prayer's been answered," she mumbled softly.

"That old man came by tonight couldn't do that for you?" he teased in a whisper.

"Probably couldn't have stuffed his soft thing into me," she said as he pulled her to her feet.

"You all right?" he asked as she tackled and hugged him.

"Sure," she said, straightening with some effort. She tossed back her hair and nodded to reassure him. In the dim light, he could see her melon-sized breasts and wondered what they would taste like.

"I'm plumb grateful for them bounty hunters," she said and pushed the hair back from her face with both hands.

He studied the graceful curve of her belly and, recalling their fiery tryst, ran his palm over it. Smooth and firm, he wanted to knead it as they kissed again. They both breathed through their noses; the intoxication began to grow again.

Gently, she pushed him back. "How long since you last ate?"

"Day or so," he lied.

"My God, I've got to feed you."

"Thought you had been."

"Oh, you—I have some new potatoes, I'll fry them."

"No—"

"Yes. You'll need your energy."

Slocum sat on a straight-back chair. She'd lighted a candle on the table for her to see by. He studied her form in the flickering light; he wasn't going to argue with her about fixing him some food. He'd sure need lots of strength if he stayed there for very long.

"Try on some of Jim's clothes. You don't mind wearing them, do you?" she asked.

"Not at all."

"Good. They should fit you." She left and returned putting on a fresh dress. "I think enough is enough. For now anyway." Then she laughed. Her hand flew to her mouth to silence herself. "I haven't laughed much lately."

"Shame," he said. "But I understand why."

She nodded and sliced more potatoes. "This and some side meat. Got some fresh whole wheat bread too."

"And butter?"

"Yes, I do, and some fig jam."

After his meal, she blew out the candle and gave her head a toss. "My bed's on the back porch."

He followed her tall form out the open door and into the screened-in porch area. She took off the dress, hung it on a hook, drew back the snowy sheet and then crawled over to the far side. Sitting up, she gathered her hair and tied it back with a ribbon. Her great melons shaking in the pearly light looked as inviting as anything for Slocum. He wanted to taste them so bad he could hardly control himself.

"I guess I was a little crazed in there." She motioned toward the kitchen.

"About right," he said, sliding on the bed and cupping her left breast in his palm.

"Hell, if you're game again, so am I." Then she gave a soft laugh as his mouth closed over the silver-dollar-sized nipple.

10

Slocum straightened his stiff back. The tarp dam across the irrigation ditch was set and should hold. He sat down on the grassy bank, washed the mud off his bare feet, dried them with some grass and replaced his socks and worn boots. Then with the long-handled shovel on his shoulder, he started back to take out the tarp set above in the field ditch and let the water come down to his new one.

A killdeer screamed at him from the waving alfalfa, chasing about after insects in the thick legumes. Slocum gave the verdant crop a critical once-over. It should make lots of rich hay for her animals or for sale. The last set taken down, the water rushed down the ditch for the next three borders with fresh-cut openings in the bank to flood them. The tarp set out to dry and the crosspiece and sticks in a neat pile, Slocum shoveled in the previous cuts. Water was three-fourths of the way down the field on them and would have enough force to run out to the end. The new set wouldn't need to be checked for another hour.

At the pump, he swept off his wide-brimmed straw hat and washed his head under the flush from the pipe. Jim had built a heck of a farm. To the north, the saw edges of the distant McDowell Mountains wavered in the heat. The cottonwoods Jim planted in the yard were already making shade. The herd of a half dozen jersey milk cows produced butter and cream, cash items for sale in the mining camps that dotted Arizona. Neat sheds, cribs and haystacks made the place a farming man's dream. The field of Mexican June corn's dried fodder rustled, the great ears already hung down in yellowing husks, close to gathering.

"My, Mr. Slocum, it sure is hot today," six-year-old Jason said from behind a mask of brown freckles topped with reddish hair.

"Hot enough, I guess."

"Ma's in the garden. I came for another basket. We've got too many beans." He held up the wicker container.

"I'll go along and help," Slocum said and they soon joined the others, busy picking green beans.

Ruby looked up, swept the curls from her face and nodded. "Sure lots of things getting ripe at once out here."

"I can see," he said and set in to help them pick. "That alfalfa is going to need to be cut next week."

"I was afraid of that."

"Why?"

"Well . . . I broke the last pitman rod on the last cutting."

"Guess we can make some more up." He looked over at her and she made a face at him: *Not now.*

He nodded that he understood and went back to picking. Whatever kept her from getting new pitman rods was something that she wanted kept from the children. The bushels filled at last, she straightened. "All right, you kids can pump the horse tank full and then you may splash in it. Slocum and I can carry the beans to the house."

The threesome left shouting, and she wiped her face on her sleeve. "Brother Yarborough owns the mercantile in Lehi."

"You're kind of avoiding him, right?"

She made a pained face at him. "Yes. He's the one the bishop thinks I should marry."

"That old skinflint bastard?" He recalled his first night in the community and the man's outrageous prices for canned tomatoes.

"Yes."

"I'll go get the wooden blanks for you and rebuild them." He picked up the bushel for her to carry full of the green beans, then with a nod to her troubled face, he sent her on. He hefted the second one by both handles and followed her down the row.

"We—me and the kids—will have plenty to eat this winter anyway. I planned to take a few bushels of beans to the social Saturday night for folks without."

"Generous of you to do that. How long can you refuse the bishop?"

"He ain't God."

"That won't make much difference. You have to live here."

"I know, and I don't want to leave. It's a great place and Jim worked hard to get it in this shape. I can manage it—"

"If the church folks leave you alone?"

She stopped at the gate and rested the bushel on her knees. "You may be right." Then she gave him a wry shake of her head. "I'll work it out somehow."

"Sure," he said and used his shoulder on the wooden gate to open it for them.

The next day, Slocum rode into Lehi. The tall, old, gnarled cottonwoods rustled in the hot wind. The plastered Lehi Ward looked unpretentious. LDS folks never built fancy sanctuaries, they wanted serviceable ones. It would serve not only as a church, but their social hall for the community. They would pray and dance inside—as well as hold meetings of the church elders. Those men would eventually bring enough pressure to bear on Ruby, making it her obligation to marry this older man.

Another large building, the ward's warehouse, where a portion of all crops and food would be set aside, was past the church. There were stored the commodities that would feed the weak and get the rest through famines and droughts. Frugal and very secular, in the past the Mormons had brought the wrath of their neighbors down upon them until they finally escaped to Utah. Now these people had begun to spread out over the desert along the rivers into Arizona. They knew Zion and how to live and to farm in a land like this.

Slocum reined his horse up before the store with the name Yarborough in black letters over the front. He hitched the bay at the rack and went inside. Clean-shaven, fresh clothes and wearing one of Jim's straw hats, perhaps the man wouldn't recognize him.

"Good afternoon, sir," Yarborough said. "You must be a stranger."

"I need four McCormack mower pitman rods."

The man, obviously well past sixty years old, nodded and stiffly came off the stool. "They run out in Phoenix?"

"Don't know, I hadn't tried there."

"Oh. Don't guess we've ever met."

Slocum shook his head. "We ain't."

"No need to be unfriendly."

"I ain't. I came to buy four—"

"I heard you the first time." Yarborough went off in a huff. He took the pitman rods down from the place on the wall and came back. "A man needing four must have some powerful thick hay to cut." He set the sticks on the counter. "Comes to three dollars."

"That's mighty high," Slocum said. "Most places charge fifty cents apiece for them."

"I know, but we don't have a railroad here. Wherever you come from, they no doubt have railroads and that means cheaper delivery prices than out here."

"No, it means folks ain't out to rob the first stranger comes in here on business."

The man started to pick up the four sticks of hardwood, and Slocum slammed down three silver dollars. "Here's your highway robbery money."

Without a word, he took the pitman rods away from Yarborough, with an exchange of hot looks, and headed for the door.

"You're lucky I let you have them—"

Slocum stopped before going out and turned back toward the man. "You're lucky that I didn't bash you over the head with them."

"Just who the hell are you?" Yarborough jerked off his apron and started around the counter.

"Stay there, old man." Slocum used the sticks to indicate where he wanted the man to remain.

"I'll have the law after you!"

"For what? Buying four pitman rods that were overpriced?" Slocum left laughing and went out to the hitch rail. He undid the reins and swung into the saddle. Still filled with rage, he set the bay off westward in a lope. He knew Yarborough was back there, staring after him; he could feel his cold eyes.

"You got in an argument with him?" she asked, sounding disbelieving coming inside the toolshed.

Slocum looked up from his work—fitting the hardware taken off each broken rod onto the new wood.

"That man is an old pirate. He charged a dollar more than they were worth."

"But I gave you three dollars. He always charges that much."

"Robbery. No competition in that burg. They ain't worth over a quarter apiece; fifty cents would make him rich."

"What did he do?"

"Got all uppity when I told him he was too high. I threatened to brain him with them."

At last, she smiled. "Well, you see why I think being married to Brother Yarborough would be no bed of roses."

"I agree."

"Guess I'll be getting more company now." She looked off in the distance from her place half inside the shed door. "They'll all need to know about the gentile in my house."

"Sorry, but that's twice the man struck me all wrong."

"Hey, I'm not blaming you—if I thought for one moment that Jim's death wasn't an accident . . ."

"You do or don't?" He'd had enough of the oven-hot shed and motioned her to go outside. "You believe it or not?"

"Jim could swim." She shook her head and threw it back to get the hair from her face.

"Who was there when it happened?"

"The one you met in town, Yancy Yarborough, Brother Cox, Markam Hanky—he works some for Yarborough— and some other men—I lost count."

"Who'd want to kill Jim?"

"Nobody, I guess. Owed no one. Course he wasn't the best Mormon in the community. Oh, he didn't drink or carouse. But if he had a job needed done, he did it first, then if there was time for church things, he did them. That ain't exactly how they like it."

"Personal things before the church?"

"Oh, they called him out on it. Jim told them to mind their own damn business."

"That was all that happened?"

"Far as I know."

She dismissed them with a head shake. "If you hadn't come along—" She looked around to be certain none of the little ones were within hearing. "I might have lost my mind anyway."

"There's always your nieghbor, Brother Cox," Slocum said, and grinned at her threatening fist.

Saturday afternoon, she bathed the children and herself. They were all going to the social, and she laid out Jim's clean clothing for Slocum to wear. He washed up at the barn and changed out there. The team was hitched, and with baskets of food for them to eat, the extra garden produce to give away and blankets in the wagon, the children were loaded in and Ruby climbed on the seat. Slocum double-checked the harness, stepped up, and they set out for Lehi.

Things were bustling when they arrived at the small crossroads. Women called out to Ruby, and others did a double take at the sight of a man with her on the spring seat. She had him park in the last shady spot available.

"Reckon gossiping tongues will wag?" he asked under his breath.

"Good," she said. "Then maybe they won't ask me again to marry an old man."

"Maybe?"

"Why, Ruby Branch." The flush faced woman swept her sunbonnet back to see them.

"Sister Carpenter, I want you to meet Jim's best friend, Slocum."

"My, isn't that nice, you coming by to help a poor widow."

"Yes, she needed some help this summer."

"Oh, then you won't be staying long?" Mrs. Carpenter asked.

"Depends," Slocum said, taking each of the three children off one at a time.

"Depends?" she asked openly.

"How long she needs me."

"I see. Well, Sister Branch, you are fortunate one of

Jim's friends dropped by. Now I must see about the punch." She shook her head. "Those sisters never make it right, if I ain't there."

"You could have been less obvious," Ruby whispered to him as the children hounded her for some hard candy.

"How?"

"I don't know, but that is the biggest blabbermouth in the valley."

"I ruined your reputation?"

"No, but Sister Carpenter is a troublemaker."

"I won't say another word."

She turned, holding her finger to her mouth to silence her brood. "I must take the children to Yarborough's. I promised to buy them some hard candy."

"Want me to go?"

"No," she said and wrinkled her nose. "They'll be busy, I can get in and out. Come on, children. Stay together, take each other's hand. There's lots of traffic."

Watching Ruby herd her wards across the dusty dirt road at last, Slocum turned to begin unhitching the team. He felt conspicuous in Jim's suit, but it fit well enough and he had nothing to hide. They could like or lump him.

"Guess we haven't met," a big man said. With a long black beard, he looked like some biblical personage.

"I wouldn't know where we'd meet," Slocum said, taking an armful of harness off the near horse.

"Baxter McCall. I was a good friend of Jim's."

"Slocum's mine."

The bareheaded man shook Slocum's hand and met his hard gaze. "Glad to meet you, and appreciate your helping her. She's a good woman."

"I'm curious," Slocum said, being certain they were alone.

"What's that?"

"Were you there when Jim drowned?"

"Why?"

Slocum shook his head. "Just curious."

"I was dragging up more logs with my team. I never saw him fall in. Heard them shout, 'A man's in the water.' "

"He ever surface?"

"No one ever saw him again," McCall said, "till we found his body three days later."

Slocum thanked him, then went to take the other harness off. Ruby and her children were coming back from the store. "You don't recall who called out?"

"I guess it was Markam Hanky."

"He a farmer from around here?"

"No. He works for Yancy Yarborough."

Slocum nodded. The pirate he disliked who the bishop wanted Ruby to marry—how damn convenient that his hired man was the last one to see Jim alive.

"You look upset," she whispered, joining him.

"Tell you later. Everyone get candy?" he asked the children, who nodded with their lips wet from licking. "Mr. McCall came by and introduced himself."

"Hello, Brother McCall."

"Good to see you."

"Need any green beans? We have several extra bushels with us."

"Ours got ate by the grasshoppers. That would sure be generous. The misses would love them."

"Good, help yourself. They're in the wagon."

"Any way I can help you?" McCall asked.

"I've got hay in a week and her corn needs shucking," Slocum said.

"We can only pay them in shares," Ruby quickly said.

"I can spare my boys. Shares'll work."

"Thanks. They're good workers," Ruby said to Slocum.

Slocum nodded. He was watching a couple of riders coming in. They weren't farmers; they looked like cowboys.

"There's Hanky now," McCall said. "He might answer your questions."

"Questions?" Ruby asked, then lowered her voice to Slocum. "Stay away from Hanky. He's Yarborough's dog. He bites."

"Him and Jim ever have words?"

"Once—why?"

Slocum shook his head to dismiss her. Even in the falling light, he could see Hanky's hard eyes under the broad-brimmed hat, surveying everything before he dismounted with a clink of his spurs.

Ruby asked to sit out the dances; might look bad for a widow to be so frivolous. Slocum agreed, but was soon jerked up and made to dance by an array of women young and old. The music was fast and the ward building soon heated up. Sweet lemonade with the luxury of ice chunks floating in it was the watering trough between sets. And each new partner posed questions to Slocum that he gave vague answers to.

"They know your life history yet?" Ruby asked casually when he bowed out and took a seat.

"Most of it."

"Not much new happens here. We get a little news from freighters and some from Salt Lake City. That's mostly church news and about the polygamy issue."

"Is there much of that here?"

"A few, but they're secret. The U.S. deputy marshal has been here checking. That's why they're so suspicious of strangers."

"I see. Is Yarborough one?"

"No. Both his wives are dead."

"Just wondered."

She nodded. "You have a new partner coming."

"Can I borrow him, Sister Branch?" the tall, thin woman in her thirties asked.

"It's up to him, Sister Kennedy."

"I'll dance," he said with a smile and rose.

She led him off. "Name's Thelma," she said under her breath.

"Slocum."

"Knew that. My place is a mile and a half south of hers. Got green porch posts. Roses in the yard. And a new windmill. You ever get an aching, come by."

"Your man?"

She winked knowingly. "He's gone with the sheep to the mountains till fall."

"I see."

"Knowed you didn't look stupid." Then the music started and he spun her away, trying to cover his amusement over her propositioning him.

At long last the last dance was over and ground cloths were spread under the wagons. Her children were already asleep in the wagon box. He and Ruby sat upon the canvas and let the night's excitement drain away.

"No fights tonight," she said, leaning back with her arms braced behind her.

"They have them?"

"Sure. Usually younger boys over some girl." She shook her head in the starlight as if amused.

"Jim took to this life and enjoyed it?" Slocum asked, finding it hard to believe his former cattle driving partner found farming that interesting, though Ruby was a big factor in it, no doubt.

"Yes, he really did. I was surprised. We came here and Jim warned me fitting in with these people would not be easy. But they wanted converts, and understood us I think."

"Long ways from Dodge City."

"Many of them would probably be shocked to death to know what I did in the past." She shook her head then threw it back. "You know I don't miss it. Never did. Jim was such a . . ."

"Strong guy. You two could have made it anywhere."

"Yes, but this place was like my home, where I was raised in Indiana. Growing things."

"We better get some sleep. They'll expect you at services. And I'll go milk the cows, then come back to get you and the kids."

"Hate to leave you with all the work."

He met her concern with a wrinkle of his nose. "Do me good to milk six cows."

"Slocum, I know you can't stay forever, but I will treasure our days."

"Don't count them."

"I won't."

"Good night." He took his cloth and blanket away a respectable distance.

Before sunup, he was up and rode back to her place. The rich smell of milk cow's manure hung on the cool morning air as he opened the barn and the placid, brindle-faced sisters went in their stanchions. He poured a scoop of ground barley in for each to eat, then set out to milk them.

He brushed off the dried dirt and grass from the first one's udder and teats. Seated on a one-legged stool, he began to squeeze the white flow out of her into a tin pail. Then the milk was strained through cheesecloth and into a tall can. He straightened his stiff back and, empty pail in hand, went on to the second one.

A noise outside from a whimpering dog made him stop the rhythmic ring of milk squirting into the bucket. He rose, hung the bucket on a nail and eased himself toward the door.

"You check the house?" the first voice asked.

"Yeah, no one there."

"After we fix these cows . . ."

Slocum drew the cap-and-ball Colt. He hoped it fired. With it in his hand, he stepped out the doorway. "Fix what cows?"

The two rannies, hardly out of their teens, stopped. One dropped a jackknife from his hand and went to stuttering. "W-who the hell are you?"

"The man who's going to fix you. Now quick, what were you going to do to her cows?"

"Nothing—"

"You've got thirty seconds, then I'm shooting off your left ear." With a deliberate move, he raised the revolver and looked down the sight.

"Don't shoot us. We was only doing what we were told." Both of them paled at the notion of his pistol pointed at them.

"Told by who?"

"Hanky."

Slocum took better aim. "What did he say to do?"

"I swear—fix them cows."

"I don't savvy 'fix' them."

"Cut their teats like they'd ran through a barbwire fence, so they couldn't be milked."

"Turn around," Slocum ordered.

"What you doing to us?"

"Taking you to the law so you can tell your story to them."

"Law—"

"Yeah, turn around." Slocum moved in and jerked out their guns. He tossed them aside on the ground. Then he took some rope and bound their hands behind their backs, making them sit on their butts and wait while he finished milking.

The can of fresh milk in the water cooler, he rounded up their horses. Then he discovered the dead collie; his anger for the pair deepened. Her pups were still acting afraid and hung back. The kids did not need to see their destroyed pet. Slocum shook his head. He took the dog by the tail and dragged it while he led the horses to the dairy shed. The carcass out of sight until he could dispose of it, he put both men on their horses, saddled the bay for himself and set out for Lehi.

"What'cha going to do to us?" the younger one kept asking, sounding scared.

"That's up to the law," Slocum said with little patience for them.

The still carcass of the collie still rested hard on his mind. A stiff, hot wind swept his face as the bay started over a plank bridge to cross the main irrigation canal. He had turned to see about his prisoners when the sharp report of a rifle sent the youngest, hard hit in the chest, face-down off his horse.

Colt in his hand, Slocum whirled around, but the next report took his second prisoner in the face and threw him off the butt of his horse. For an instant, in the distance, Slocum spotted a hatless figure with a rifle raising up, then fleeing over the dirt mound beyond the big canal. Nothing he could do about him—at the distance, his pistol would be worthless.

He dropped off the bay and found both of the young men were dead. The shots were perfect—one in the heart, the other in the face with a high-caliber, probably a .44/.40 or some game rifle. Filled with a new resolve to settle the matter, Slocum looked again at the dirt pile beyond the main canal. Perhaps a spent cartridge on the ground over there would tell him more.

Those two were silenced forever. They wouldn't implicate Hanky or Yarborough. He caught their horses and loaded the bodies—he would need a story. It would go like this: he caught them burglaring her home and was bringing them in. He planned to mention nothing they said about Hanky's orders. Folks might know the pair. But he didn't. Let the chips fall—he started for Lehi again.

He could hear the hymn being sung, the old pipe organ playing, when he reined up out in front. The double doors were open and someone looked out at him when he dismounted. Then three men rushed outside.

"What's happened here?"

"You tell me," Slocum said. "Who were they?"

"Victor and Bobbie Yount, cowhands. Who shot them?"

"Better question."

"You?"

"No. I was bringing them in for the burglary of Mrs. Branch's house."

"Burglary? Then who shot them?"

"Some dry gulcher from across the canal."

"Why?"

"Simple enough, I reckon—so they couldn't talk."

"Talk about what?"

"Damned if I know," Slocum said and looked up as Ruby came running from the crowd on the steps, calling his name.

11

The deputy sheriff rode out from Mesa. A mustached, bowlegged man in his forties, who removed his hat for Ruby and exposed his snow white forehead. Slocum saw him from the granary, where he and the teenage McCall boys were unloading a load of corn ears. Slocum excused himself to go and see about the lawman.

Eyes harder than chunks of coal, the shorter man nodded when Ruby introduced him. "Slocum, this is Mike Dulvain. He's from the sheriff."

"Howdy. You were the one taking them two in?"

"Yeah, taking them to Lehi anyway. Had no way to know where the law was in this country, being a stranger."

"Well, we ain't got much. You own a rifle?"

"No, sir."

Dulvain nodded. "Someone took them out of here with a forty-four-forty. That's what Doc said when he looked them over. You ever see them two before?" The lawman looked at both of them.

"No."

"Guess they were drifters. Thinking everyone was in church, they picked her place." Then the deputy said something that took Slocum aback: "No one else around here knows them either."

"What do you need?' Slocum asked, ready to say the townsfolk sure had turned stupid in twenty-four hours. But he was willing to play along awhile longer and keep his mouth shut. "I can take you to where they were shot off their horses."

Dulvain shook his head. "Tracks be too cold by now. Don't like it, but justice's been served. I'd say the case was closed. Good day, ma'am, and you too, Slocum." He tipped his hat and headed for his horse.

Slocum shared a quick look at Ruby. Everyone in Lehi knew that the pair worked for Hanky—actually Yarborough. Yet they'd told Dulvain that they didn't know the two dead men?

"No one knew them?" he hissed. She wet her full bottom lip and quickly nodded. "They've closed ranks," Slocum said with disgust.

She shrugged. "We're clannish at times."

"Guilty or not, they deserved a trial. They were shot and killed to shut them up."

"Dulvain's still in sight." She tossed her curly reddish hair after the deputy standing in the stirrups with his long-maned blue roan in a long trot.

"He can't hear us. Are they testing me?"

"Who knows. Slocum, don't be too hard on the rest of us, please?"

He knew what she meant. The others besides Yarborough—the God-fearing folks who believed in the Angel Moroni and his message for them in the book of Moroni. Yarborough used his affiliation with the church to assert his authority and his power over them. They went along with him because they probably owed money at his store and the brotherhood as well.

"What will we do with all this corn?" she asked, hugging his arm and swinging on it.

"I want to ride up to Fort McDowell and see if the agency will buy some."

"I better ask the bishop," she said in a small voice.

"Why?"

"We usually market together."

"You mean you let Yarborough market it for all of you and he gets the cream?"

"Everyone works together—that's how we do it."

"Except Jim?"

"How did you know that?"

"I drove cattle herds to Kansas for three years with your late husband. He'd never be compromised into some deal when it came to his own business."

"You're right." She dropped her gaze to the ground.

"Did they push him off that dam for that?"

Her face paled under the brown tan and she looked big-eyed at Slocum. The front edge of her even teeth sunk deep into her full lip. "Oh God, I hope not."

Buddy and Shilo McCall were driving the team up the drive toward them. The sounds of their hooves on the hard-baked ground and the jingle of the harness chains rang out. They already had the wagonful of corn un loaded.

"We can talk more tonight," he said, determined to sell as much of the crop as she could spare to the Army for cash money.

"Get a drink of water," Slocum said to the boys. "We've got time for one more load this afternoon."

"I'll get you some fresh-baked bread and butter," Ruby said and hurried off to the house.

"Lot's of corn to gather out there," the freckle-faced Buddy said and then followed his brother to the pump.

"We'll get it," Slocum said after them. And get her a fair price for it too, he thought. And the alfalfa hay he planned to cut after the corn harvest, that too could be sold. Considering her supply, it needed to be sold as surplus—he didn't need Yarborough to be the broker either.

The corn harvest required the rest of the week. At night, Slocum sharpened the two sickle bars that fit the McCormack mower, so it was greased and ready to cut the following Monday. Noon Saturday, they had the last wagon load under cover. Ruby paid the boys, man's wages in cash, and let them go home to get cleaned up for the dance that night.

The two boys rode their thin-framed Indian ponies home bareback, waving as they trotted away. The small children were still excited about the boys' departure and chattered at their mother.

"How much corn do we have?" she asked, marking down the wages in her ledger.

"Over two thousand bushels by my calculation," Slocum said, sitting on the straight-back chair.

"At thirty cents a bushel—"

"That's the price he pays for it?"

"Why? What do you think it's worth?"

"Two cents a pound."

"That's a dollar fifty a bushel of ear corn?" She looked shocked.

"The Army pays that all the time, for weevil-infested, sorry corn."

"This isn't sorry corn?"

"No, it's first grade. Should bring a premium."

"But we don't have—"

"We can hire wagons and drivers. Cash isn't that plentiful up here." Slocum stood up and looked past the wind-billowing sheer curtains at the distant purple McDowell Mountains. "That money would allow you to hire a man or two for this place."

"I can—"

"How much corn will you need for cornmeal and for fattening a few pigs to butcher this fall?"

She shrugged when he turned to look at her. "Perhaps

a hundred fifty bushels— Well, I must give the warehouse two hundred bushels too."

"Good, I can sell seventeen hundred bushels to the Army or whoever."

"Perhaps—I better talk to Bishop Fletcher about it tonight."

"You getting weak knees, girl?"

"Slocum—whatever you say. I can use the money for improvements and expenses. I'll merely mention it to him."

"Fletcher?"

"Yes, he's a good enough man."

The children were bathed and dressed. Ruby lined them up on a bench and went to get ready herself. Slocum retired to the barn for his bath and clean-up. He carried the Colt with him at all times, ever since the two invaders showed up. He had no doubt but that if they'd tried it once, they'd try it again.

At Lehi, Slocum kept the children occupied in the shade of a gnarled cottonwood, while Ruby went to talk to the bishop. He felt out of place, but enjoyed the good humor of the children, who were all set to go on a promised candy raid when their mother returned from her business.

She came back frowning. "I can't sell the corn."

"What?" he snorted out loud and then looked around to see who had overheard his outburst. He lowered his voice. "Why not?"

She swallowed. "Others have lower grade corn and theirs would be harder to sell without mine. The plan is to blend the ward's corn together and thus get a higher price for everyone."

"Harder for who to sell, Yarborough?"

She nodded like a schoolgirl. "He's handling the sale for the ward."

"Not your corn!" He shook his head. "Can't you see he's taking all the profit?"

"It's for the good—"

"For the good of that old tyrant. No, I'm handling this for you."

"Slocum, please. I have to live here."

"Where is this bishop?" He searched around for the man.

"Slocum, please don't cause a scene." She clutched his arm.

He stopped and looked hard at the mountains. Then he nodded. "Take the children for their candy."

"What are you going to do?"

"Wait here."

"You'll not—not here and not tonight?" she asked, but he didn't answer her, until at last he shrugged away her concern.

"I'll repay you," she said in a grateful gush and then spoke to the children. "Take each other's hand. There's lots of traffic."

12

Slocum saddled the bay long before sunup Monday morning. He left her a note, to have the boys start cutting the hay, he'd be back by dark. In the predawn, he trotted his pony through Lehi and up the river road for Fort McDowell. Middle of the morning, he pulled over the pass and could see the green line of cottonwoods in the basin beneath him. The big horse was holding up fine—snorting and his shoulders wet with sweat from the growing heat, but he had mended at Ruby's on the good hay and grain.

The first place Slocum stopped to check was the adobe headquarters under the flagpole. A private stood guard and challenged him.

"Looking for the quartermaster," Slocum said.

"That's me," a uniformed man in his forties said, coming outside.

"You needing some good corn?"

"Fodder or food?"

"Food quality, that's for certain."

"I never caught your name?"

Slocum swept off his straw hat and introduced himself.

"Lewis is mine."

Then Slocum showed him a couple of ears in the shuck

121

from his saddlebags. The officer stripped the husk back and looked hard at the flat, thick kernels on the cob. He wrenched the corn in both hands, and the pale golden grain spilled into his palms. He took a grain and chewed on it. With a nod of satisfaction, he smiled.

"It's sweet even."

"How much can you buy?"

"How much of this can you deliver?" Lewis closed one eye to squint out of the other at Slocum.

"Fifteen hundred bushel."

"All this good?"

"It's been picked and in the shed."

"I'd give you three and a third cents a pound for it here."

Slocum nodded that he had heard the man. Absently, he looked across the empty parade ground as a small dust devil swirled through the area and disappeared in the direction of the walled tents. That third of a cent might pay for the haul. Whether the church officials liked it or not, he was going to make Jim's last crop bring a good price for her.

"I can't buy that much corn that good up here."

"Wouldn't be that a certain man won't sell it to you?"

Lewis smiled and nodded. "All I usually have to deal with. You mean Yancy Yarborough?"

Slocum gave a bob of his head.

"Them Mormons won't like you meddling in their business."

"Some will and some won't," Slocum said with a grin. He'd already lined up four men to help him haul the corn.

"What's good alfalfa worth here?" Slocum asked.

"Been paying two cents. You have some?"

"I'll have thirty tons coming in the next two weeks."

"Alfalfa?"

"Straight, cleanest hay you've bought."

The two men shook hands. Lewis offered Slocum some

food, but he politely refused. He had the McCall boys at home mowing hay that day. He needed to get back and be sure all was well there.

"You have a deal, Captain. First corn will arrive in a few days."

"I'll be ready and looking forward to working with you."

"I've got a friend up here used to scout for the Army. Dirty Shirt Jones? You know him?"

"Yes, he rode out yesterday to catch some wild horses. He should be back anytime."

"Tell him Slocum was by and will be back."

"I'll do that."

Slocum saluted the man, mounted his horse and headed west. It would be late in the day when he returned to Ruby's place. On purpose he scouted around Lehi and came in the back way. No need in Yarborough guessing what he was up to—until it was too late. With the sun low in the west, he set the bay off on the steep escarpment trail that led to the green valley below; he felt satisfied his plan would work.

"Where have you been?" she asked, out of breath.

"Never mind, it would only upset you. I want you to take some ears of your corn to Yarborough and find out how much he will pay for it."

"But—"

"I'm going along. He won't try anything."

"No trouble?"

"No trouble. You will show him the quality and then ask for his best price. I won't say a thing."

"Oh, do I have to?" She furrowed her brow at him.

"Yes."

They asked Shilo to watch the children; Buddy was to cut more hay. They drove the two seater with the bay in the traces to Lehi.

The corn ears in a cloth bag over her arm, Ruby let

Slocum help her down. Skirt in hand, she led the way toward the open doorway. He could read the hesitation, but he smiled away her concern and she went inside.

Yarborough glanced over from his bookkeeping, then waved the clerk away who had set down his broom to come wait on her. Yarborough planned to handle her himself. He rose from his chair, but not with the spring he wanted to demonstrate, no doubt for her.

"Aw, Sister Branch." He nodded to acknowledge Slocum. "What brings you to town on this bright day? Surely there must be many things for a widow to do on such a large farm."

"My farm is fine." She set the cloth bag on the counter with a clunk. "I have come to have you tell me what my corn is worth."

"Oh, yes, business." The man squared his shoulders as if to get in a businesslike mood. He looked at Slocum, then at her. With his gold-rimmed glasses making him look like a boy peeking under a circus tent, he lifted the edge of the material and removed an ear.

"Weights good." He hefted it in his palm.

She nodded. Slocum remained with his arms folded, a few feet back, awaiting the man's appraisal.

"You have a nice ride yesterday?" he asked Slocum without looking up.

"Yes, I did."

"Versatile horse. I see he's in harness today." Yarborough nodded toward the front window.

Slocum merely bobbed his head as the merchant stripped away the dry shuck. The immediate look in his eyes was one of greed when he exposed the grain. In a thousand card games, Slocum had seen men dealt king-high flushes before. Then the look melted and his mouth formed a straight line.

"Nice enough, but average corn for this valley. Jim wasted his money. May his soul rest in peace, but that high-priced seed he bought and imported wasn't any better than the brand that I sell here."

"How much a pound?" Ruby asked.

"Oh, it's too pale-colored. Not yellow like they like. I guess around a penny and a half would be my very best offer. I'm sorry, Sister Branch. I know your little ones—"

"My little ones are fine. They are of no concern of yours. Is that your final price?"

Yarborough shook his head as if he had done all he could do. "If it was real yellow-colored even—I might give a quarter cent more. But it is so pale."

He took off his glasses, and his weak eyes squinted at Slocum as if for some support on this issue. "You know the best grade of corn is yellow?"

"Ready?" Slocum asked Ruby softly, ignoring the man's question.

She nodded sharply, gathering the corn and the bag.

"I can start receiving it anytime. I'll pay twenty percent down on delivery, twenty in six months and the balance next year at planting time. I know you will need my seed for next year's crop, since this expensive seed didn't do the job this year."

"We will be back in touch," Slocum said and thanked the man.

Ruby seemed devastated. Shaking her head as if very disappointed, she rushed out in the sunshine. Slocum hurriedly helped her into the wagon, rushed around, undid the brake and left Yarborough on the dock, shouting how sorry he was that her corn was such poor quality.

"Poor quality!" she finally said through her gritted teeth. "If my corn's so poor then they don't need it to mix with the others' grain. Take it to the fort and sell it for that price!"

"Yes, ma'am," Slocum said and reined down the bay to cross the bridge where the two were shot. "We can do that."

• • •

The next day, Slocum and Shilo took the last picked
wagon load of corn from the shed to Lehi, to put it in the
warehouse. Buddy continued the mowing. Ruby assured
Slocum that the doors to the warehouse would be unlocked and they could shovel the corn into the bin. When
they reined up behind the building, Shilo jumped down
to undo the door. It bore a fresh padlock on the hasp and
the youth frowned at Slocum.

"She said it would be open."

Then someone from Yarborough's store came on the
run. Slocum tossed his head toward the runner.

"Who's that?"

"Micheal McGee, he works for Yancy."

"Mr. Yarborough said he wants the corn unloaded over
there," the swaggering boy announced.

Slocum jumped down from the wagon. "This is tithe
corn. It isn't for sale. It goes in the warehouse."

"That ain't what Mr Yarborough said."

"He lock this door?" Slocum motioned toward it.

"I sure don't know. He said for me to tell you—"

"He in charge of this warehouse?" Slocum turned the
lock over in his hand.

"He told me to—"

With the butt of his pistol, Slocum smashed the lock
and it fell open. He tossed it aside like a dead bug, and
as if McGee was nowhere around, he spoke to Shilo.
"Let's get to shoveling."

A quick check inside showed the bin near empty as
Slocum holstered his revolver. He excused himself and
went around the red-faced McGee to climb on the wagon.

"We need to get this over with," he said to Shilo, who
already was bouncing shovels of corn ears off the floor
inside.

"You don't disobey Mr. Yarborough's orders and get
away with it!" McGee shouted and stomped his foot.

"You go over there and tell that Mr. Yarborough this is tithe corn, and he wants any, he can buy it for four bucks a bushel at Ruby Branch's place."

"Four bucks a bushel? Why . . . why that's robbery."

"Yes, and there ain't much left at that price." Slocum shared a private grin with the boy on the other shovel.

McGee hurried back to the store. Slocum kept an eye out for someone else to come by and tell him where to put the corn. No one came and they soon had the load in the warehouse bin. Finished, they drank water from their canteen, then they took turns pouring some on each other's head and neck to cool off.

"About time we headed home," Slocum said, pulling the bin door shut.

A bearded man drove up in a light buggy and with a frown came hurrying up.

"Bishop Fletcher," Shilo said under his breath.

Slocum nodded. "Glad you got here, Reverend. We've just got the first load of corn in the bin. Ruby's ten percent. Don't reckon we need a receipt, but you can look in there and agree. It's over fifty bushels. I figure the two hundred will cover her tithe."

"Yes, ah, yes." Fletcher looked around and especially toward Yarborough's.

"Sorry about the lock, but no one here had a key, so I busted it open. Didn't figure anyone was lowlife enough to steal from a church anyway."

"That's—" he swallowed hard, "quite all right."

He stepped in the door and picked up an ear. He peeled the shuck back and looked in dismay at the grain on the cob.

"Some corn, isn't it?"

"My, yes, but how—"

"Missus told me that Jim special ordered this seed from Tucson. Comes from a hacienda in Sonora."

"Yes, I understood it was quite expensive."

"We figured that the crop made fifty bushels per acre. That cheapened the seed some."

"Fifty bushels?"

"That's what she based the tithe on. If we underestimated it, we will bring the rest."

"You are selling it to Yarborough, aren't you?"

Slocum shook his head. "He's only paying a cent and a half. Said hers was too poor quality to pay that much for it even. So she didn't want it ruining the rest of the ward's corn. You understand—Yarborough said it was such a poor grade corn."

"Yes, but who will you sell it to?" The bishop's voice went up two octaves.

Slocum climbed on the seat, took up the reins. "I know you share my concern for Jim's widow and those little children and their welfare."

"Of course, but . . . but we all work together—"

"I know. And Mr. Yarborough over there, he gets richer with each crop."

"He has been fair—"

The reins in his hands, Slocum kicked off the brake. "We get through, if that isn't ten percent that we shoveled in there, we will make up the difference. Good day, Bishop."

"No trouble at the warehouse?" Ruby asked, acting anxious as she walked alongside the wagon when they came up the drive.

"It's in the warehouse and the bishop acknowledged it. Said it was the best corn he'd ever seen."

"What else?"

"We discussed the price of corn." Slocum reined up, handed the lines to Shilo. "Put them ponies up." Then he jumped down and hugged her shoulder. "Quit worrying."

"If that old tyrant had even offered me anything for that corn—I'd have sold to him."

"You tried. The wagons will be here in the morning to begin to haul it to the fort."

"He might try to stop you." She frowned at him.

"Paying a half a cent a pound freight is robbery, but it will be hard for him to dissuade any of those men who are bringing their wagons from doing it."

"I hope it works."

He hugged her to his chest.

"It will, Ruby."

Three more loads shoveled into the warehouse later, he looked off to the red-stained sky in the west. Hay came next.

Men and their wagons began to arrive before daylight. Slocum and the McCall boys helped them load out. He figured the average farm wagon would hold close to fifty bushels with side boards on the box. That meant thirty wagon loads to the fort. With fifteen various farmers pledged to freight the corn, Slocum knew it would require two trips. At two days per trip, most of the men begged to separate the hauls by a week, and Slocum had agreed.

Men scurried around in the predawn. McCall caught him by the sleeve.

"There's plenty of shovelers," the man assured him. "How did the trip to Lehi go yesterday?"

"Someone put a lock on the door."

"Lock on the ward warehouse?"

"I busted it. Then a boy named McGee told me to deliver it to Yarborough."

McCall shook his head. "The bishop acted upset last night about this business of selling it at the fort."

"I spoke to him too. Yarborough cooked his own goose when he said her corn was too substandard. Too pale to sell, he told her."

"I can warn you, Slocum." McCall looked around.

"That shooter that killed those two—I figure he's still out there."

Slocum nodded his head, then he spoke to a man pulling up his loaded rig ahead so the next one could fill his. "We'll be loaded and ready to go in thirty minutes."

He watched Ruby going about serving fresh bread and orange juice. The one item he missed the most among these people, coffee—a taboo for Mormons. They'd be on the road shortly, with safety in their numbers.

"You boys dump-rake the dry hay today," he instructed the two McCall boys. "Rake it into small shocks, and it will keep till we can haul it. Quit for the day when it gets so dry that the leaves begin to shatter."

Both agreed. He hurried off to put his things in his own rig, which was already loaded.

"Be careful, Slocum," she whispered. "I packed enough food in there for you to eat."

"You watch careful too," he said, not daring to kiss her in such company.

"I will," she promised and he left.

13

Slocum drove the lead wagon. A half hour later they jogged through Lehi. A few cur dogs chased them, but no one came out of the Yarborough store. Along the way various wives and family members waved at them from their yard gates. Children ran beside, shouting and laughing for a short distance.

Over and over in Slocum's mind, he went through the possibilities of how Yarborough would try to stop them. And he would try, since his underhanded efforts in the guise of the community's best interests had been exposed. Yarborough was too tough to let this threat to his business go unanswered.

A vision of the shooter picking off those two with deadly accuracy still chilled him. An unnamed killer out there somewhere, and if he had any money, he'd bet the gunner was associated with the businessman. Under the hot sun, Slocum shook his head to try and dismiss his concerns. Half her corn crop was on the way to Fort McDowell.

In late afternoon, they pulled down the long grade. Slocum felt the relief ease his shoulders. No breakdowns, no crippled horses, not an incident. Indian dogs rushed out to bark at them. Wide brown eyes spied on them from grass-thatched wickiups. Curious women looked up from grinding corn in metates. Squatted men in loincloths and regular shirts nodded as they spoke of the passing train.

Captain Lewis came out of headquarters and shook his head as if amazed.

"When you do business, you get on with it," he said, looking up at Slocum.

With a nod, he set the brake and clamored off the seat. "Good to see you, sir."

They shook hands.

"You must have got up early."

"We did. These're neighbors, helping out a widow woman."

Lewis nodded. "I suppose they want to unload and head back?"

"Sure would help. They all have farms to tend."

"Sergeant, get a light. Cooler to work by night anyway," Lewis said.

"Thanks."

The scales were checked and balanced. Then a wagon was driven up on them, weighed, unloaded, reweighed and the price computed. At a half a cent per pound, as Slocum had figured, the freighters would earn over seventeen dollars apiece for their haul. It was obvious too from the start that the corn weighed well and that her portion of the sale would be over three thousand dollars. A fortune in a cash-thin society where the freighters' individual incomes from the two hauls might clear most of their personal debts.

"Sure beats what Yarborough pays to freight a load of grain up here," McCall said to Slocum in the bug-sizzling night.

"How much he pay?"

"Four dollars a trip."

Slocum chuckled. "Guess that's why I got so many to answer my request."

"Sure is."

Near midnight, the weary teamsters dropped into their bedrolls. The camp soon was a-buzz with snores. Slocum had drank some coffee with Lewis and was savoring the richness of this luxury.

"This half of it?" Lewis asked.

"Close to it."

"Watch your back," Lewis said.

"I do."

Lewis nodded. "There's word out this trading won't last."

Slocum nodded and then took another sip of coffee. "I suspected that much."

He stared across the dayroom at the plastered adobe wall and a picture of President Cleveland. Going against the grain never set well; his problem was to know when it would explode and how to be ready for it.

The teamsters returned home the next day, a little less jubilant than at the start and road-worn as they split off for their own places. Slocum waved to them and drove on. The bright afternoon sun on him, he wiped his sweaty face on his sleeve. He rumbled the wagon across the canal bridge and wondered about the shooter—he felt easier at last going up her driveway and hearing the dead collie's pups barking at him.

Skirt in her hand, Ruby rushed out of the house and through the gate. "You're back and safe."

"And—" He held up the heavy canvas sack containing the money for the corn. The team halted and she climbed on the wheel.

"How much?"

"Three thousand, one hundred and thirteen dollars."

Her face paled. "My God." Her hand went to her lips. "Sorry, but that's a fortune."

"Half the corn crop."

"Really? Oh, I had never dreamed of so much money."

"That don't count the hay either."

She shook her head and slipped back to the ground. "Jim said planting the corn after alfalfa would do that." With a disappointed shake of her head, she dropped her gaze. "If only he was here to share this with us."

For a long moment, Slocum considered her words. "He's looking down and proud of us."

With glistening eyes, she looked up at him. "Yes, he is."

Things went slower. Slocum found a freighter in Mesa to haul the hay. The farmers were busy with their own crops; taking time for the second corn haul was about all they could spare. The freighter had oxen teams and three double wagons that he promised to fit with hay racks. At thirty cents per hundred weight, they shook hands.

The McCall boys lined up the help of several other teen boys to load the hay when the teamsters arrived. Slocum grew more edgy when the last corn haul was completed. Nothing had happened from the competition.

Working on shaping a new tongue for the wagon, since the present one showed some dry crack, he used a draw knife on the blank Jim had drying in the shop loft.

He looked up when the bearded face of Bishop Fletcher appeared. For a moment he thought of the cross-draw holster in his lap. The man should be no threat. He nodded to him and went back to pulling the draw knife and shaving off wood.

"I am here to ask your intentions toward Sister Ruby," Fletcher announced.

"Intentions?"

"We are a Christian community. It is not appropriate that a single man stays at the home of a widow woman."

Slocum chuckled. "Better that a married man did that?"

"What do you mean?"

"Several have been coming by."

"What do you mean by that?"

"Several saints been here with less than saintly intentions."

"Polygamy is recognized in our religion."

"So is a hard dick. I have no intentions toward Ruby. We are friends and have been for years. Her husband and I were partners in the cattle driving business before they came here." Slocum sighted down the side of the tongue. Then he took another draw off the side. "Do I make you nervous, Reverend?"

"We are a community, close-knit. By working together, we will survive."

"By letting Yarborough make all the money. Is that how you plan to continue?"

"Obviously you have no respect for the others. Brother Yancy feeds them between crops, loans them seed money. He is an essential person in this place."

"No, he's a parasite."

"You, of course, are entitled to your own opinion."

"How much do you owe him?" Slocum asked then drew in a deep inhale.

"That's—"

"None of my business. You're paying fifteen percent interest?"

"That's none of your business."

"What if I could get you a loan for ten percent?"

Fletcher's eyes looked wide open and he stepped back in a state of shock and disbelief. "How?"

"Sister Branch."

"She can't—"

"Folks been paying off Yarborough pretty regular these last few days."

"I've heard nothing of this."

"Oh, Brother Yancy never mentioned that when he sent you out here to learn of 'my intentions'?"

"He never—"

"How big is your loan?"

"That is none of your business." Fletcher turned on his heel and stomped away.

In a few minutes, he left in his buggy at a high rate of speed. Slocum went back to his work. Fletcher was an annoying horsefly; Yarborough had tougher ones.

"What did the bishop want?" she asked, coming in the shop.

"Wanted to know when we were getting married."

She blinked at him. "He what?"

"You heard me," he said, getting up and putting an arm on her shoulder. "We're shocking the community."

She grasped his hand and nodded. "Good thing they don't know about Dodge, isn't it?"

"Yes, for he acted like my presence here presented real problems. Seems I'm ruining your reputation."

"If it prevents my marrying some old man, good."

"No. I can't stay much longer. They'll hear of me and come looking."

"The bounty hunters?"

"Yes."

"There is so much here to do—"

"You can handle it. We've broken Yarborough's hold on the community."

"I don't know about this banker role."

"McCall and the others will help you."

She nodded. "When will you have to leave?"

He shrugged. "I can't tell you. I'll stay as long as I can."

"Good." She dropped her voice to a whisper. "Let's work on my wicked reputation later tonight when everyone is asleep."

He chuckled and nodded.

14

Slocum stood in the barn's shadows. His fingers closed around the butt of his Colt. The pups had been doing some sporadic barking at the house. Like perhaps a coyote was about the place and the youthful dogs were uncertain about challenging him or not. They would bark then run for cover.

After a while, lying on his back and listening, Slocum decided that it wasn't a coyote bothering the pups. He got up from the cot in the hallway of the barn where he slept. With some stuffing, he made the bed look like he was still sleeping in it under a blanket. The Colt in his hand, he moved to the front opening to the hallway.

One of the pups yapped toward the southwest. Slocum noted the direction. Who or whatever was out there was making its way around the place. Who was it? Did they want him? Memories of the Radamacher and Delaware surprise attack at Rosa's caused goose bumps on the back of his arms.

In the darkness, he eased himself close to the wall to try and get a chance to see the intruder. Step by step, he made steady, quiet progress. His heart raced and his palms grew wet with perspiration. His ears so strained they rang. Then he heard the unmistakable sound of a shotgun's hammers being locked back, followed by two ear-shattering shots.

The shooter had blasted his cot with both barrels. Slocum whirled to go back from the doorway to the alleyway, and began firing at the retreating silhouette. A cry in the night and the bushwhacker went down.

"I'm hit! I'm hit! Don't shoot."

"Get up," Slocum ordered.

"Can't—"

"You try anything, I'll blast you to hell," Slocum warned. Behind he could hear Ruby calling out to him from the back porch.

"Slocum? What's happening?"

"I'm fine! Stay there!" He could make out the man on the ground. "That you, McGee?"

"My leg. I'm bleeding to death."

"So are my blankets. Where in the hell is that greener?"

"Dropped it."

"Yarborough send you?"

"No."

"Who did?"

"I just wanted to stop you—" Then McGee moaned in pain and gripped his leg in both hands. "I'm dying—"

"Stop me from what?" Slocum jerked him up by his shirt.

"Ruining our whole community."

"Bullshit, Yarborough sent you."

"No, no, he didn't know anything about it. He's gone to his ranch above Fort McDowell."

"What's going on?" Ruby asked, holding the lamp up.

"McGee here came out to shoot me to save the community, he says."

"What's he talking about?" she asked as McGee moaned about his leg.

"He says I'm ruining the community."

"Oh, my God. What should we do now?"

"Get that deputy out of Mesa. Give him McGee. He

tried to murder someone. That's obvious." Both McCall boys were there by then.

"Your blankets were on fire from the shot," Shilo said. "We put them out."

"Good. You two carry McGee up to the house. We'll doctor his leg and then you two can take him to Deputy Dulvain in Mesa come first light."

They nodded.

"What are you going to do?" she asked.

"Go confront Yarborough. This punk don't do anything unless that man tells him to. He's covering up. That's why Yarborough went to his ranch tonight, so no one could say he killed me. Only thing wrong, he should have sent a tougher guy to do it." Slocum shook his head, wondering what the big man would try next.

"McGee here," he continued, "couldn't get up his nerve and kept them pups barking every time he got close to the yard."

"I thought it was coyotes sneaking around for a hen," she said.

"We need to pack him?" Shilo asked.

"Yes, you two take him to the house. And put him on the porch. Ruby doesn't need all that blood on her kitchen floor."

"Easy, easy," McGee complained as they picked him up.

"Yeah, you ought to be strung up," Shilo said, and both boys took the complaining shooter toward the house.

"I better saddle the bay," he said to her.

"But we—I need you."

"Things will work out. He can't deny ordering this attempted killing. Everyone knows that McGee is his flunky. I want to confront him."

"Don't do it for my sake," she said in a small voice.

"Maybe for everyone's sake. He's hid behind the facade of helping you all. He's been everyone's friend and robbed them. I figure Jim knew that too."

She closed her eyes and shook her head. "I hope you're wrong."

"Me too." He blew out the light and then kissed her hard on the mouth.

"If I can't come back, you will understand?"

"Yes," she said in a hushed voice.

"Good."

"I'll do what I can for his leg."

"I hate to leave you with a mess."

"The McCall boys and I can handle it."

Slocum squeezed her shoulder in a hug and then went for the bay. A lump in his throat, he jerked his saddle and pads off the rack in the barn. It would never be easy to leave her—damn, he better go confront Yarborough and get on his way.

She fixed him some food to take along in a poke. After a short conversation with the boys on how to handle the prisoner, he mounted up and left. Trotting the bay down the starlit driveway, he knew this would be his last visit to her place. Then the sad notion rode heavy on his mind. Thoughts about her volumptious body and passionate ways roiled his guts and only made the separation that much harder. He booted the bay into a lope.

Dawn, he located Dirty Shirt Jones's wickiup on the Fort McDowell reservation. The Yavapai came out rubbing the sleep from his eyes with his fists. He blinked his brown eyes when he looked up to see who it was.

"Goddamn, Slocum. What you doing here?"

"Looking for Yarborough's place."

Jones nodded his head. "Lehi—got a store."

"No, his ranch."

"Oh, it's just an old shack, couple cowboys hang out. Got a few cows."

"Where?"

"Up the Verde." He gave a toss of his head to the north,

then combed his coarse black hair through his fingers.

"You guiding these days?" Slocum asked.

"Sure. You paying?"

Slocum grinned and told him yes.

Jones saddled a hammer-headed gray and they headed north up the river road under the giant cottonwoods that lined the stream.

"Why are you so interested in this Yarborough's place?" Jones finally asked.

"He sent a man to kill me last night."

"Oh." Jones nodded his head as if he understood.

"We've been having a small war in Lehi. I kinda broke up his playhouse."

"That's where all that grain and hay's been coming from up here?"

"Yeah, I been getting folks top money for their crops, especially Jim Branch's widow. You know him?"

"Not real well. He was the one drowned?"

"Yes. I'm suspicious about that too."

"How you going to prove anything?"

"I been thinking on that all night riding out here. Suppose I told Yarborough I had a witness who saw Jim pushed?"

"He's a tough old bird." Jones shook his head. "And you get a Mormon jury, they'd turn him loose anyway."

"I've already learned about that," Slocum said and set his horse into a long trot. Jones kept his up beside him.

"Why is he up at his ranch?" Jones asked.

"So he'd have an alibi when I was shot."

"Sounds like you got that bunch all riled up."

"Not near riled enough." If Yarborough had anything to do with Jim Branch's death, he wanted the man to pay. But how would they ever know? Perhaps if he could separate Markam Hanky from his boss. He'd try anything to hear the truth about his ex-partner's death, accident or murder.

They rode the dim wagon road under the shade of mesquites and cottonwoods that paralleled the west side of the rushing Verde. The distant purple tops of Four Peaks were to the east, and the back side of the McDowells reared to the west. They passed several small wickiups and the diamond eyes of bare-ass brown children followed their passage.

The sun was at its zenith when Jones pointed to the left and Slocum could see that the narrow buggy wheels that had tracked from the fort took that turn. Without much sleep and with the solar heat of the desert, Slocum thought about slapping himself to stay awake.

"How much further?" he asked.

"Short ways," Jones said.

"Can we slip up on them?"

"Sure."

Jones took off through the chaparral, and Slocum followed him. In the lead, the ex-scout used a cow trail, and soon they were making a circle to reach the place. At last, he reined up and pointed through the lacy mesquite to a small gray board shack.

"There."

Slocum nodded and dismounted. The shack was hardly a big ranch house, like he'd originally expected to find, but the buggy was there and there were horses in the corral.

"Let's get up close and see what we can learn."

Jones nodded and they began to move in on the place. Slocum drew out his cap-and-ball pistol and carried it in his fist. Jones brought a single-shot carbine, a short model made for mounted soldiers. At the back of the corral, both men crouched down and tried to listen for any voices.

". . . Riley will be here in two days with those cattle. Get the brands changed and turn them out to heal."

That was Yarborough's voice giving Hanky instructions as he came outside the shack. Slocum and Jones both bellied down hard to be unseen. No doubt Yarborough would be coming for his horse. If they could only go undiscovered.

The animal obviously was ready to return to his stables at Lehi. He went to the gate and Yarborough tossed on the harness.

"You reckon that Slocum's dead?" Hanky asked from the doorway.

"How could he miss with a shotgun?" Yarborough busied himself clicking the harness in place.

"McGee ain't much, he may talk."

"He won't in court. Quit worrying. The one who spoiled our sales to the Army is dead. We can get on with our business now."

"Riley and his gang going to help change the brands?"

"No, hire a couple of cowboys. Maybe some blanket-assed ones off the reservation. They don't talk like that last two."

"They didn't talk long."

"No, you were damn lucky. Slocum had gotten you that morning, we'd've all been in duck soup."

"I handled it."

"That's why I pay you so well," Yarborough said as if growing impatient.

Slocum heard him step up on the wagon with a creak. So Hanky had been there that morning too, slipping around and taking out the pair so they couldn't testify. What about Jim's death? Slocum lay on the sandy ground as close to the base of the corral as he could get. Luckily for him, the corral was a series of rotten poles stacked up, and enough old ones filled the bottom two feet to conceal him and Jones.

"You get those cattle done, come on down to Lehi. We'll discuss who else needs a lesson."

"When we got rid of Branch, I thought the rest would figure it out."

"There's still some other resistance. Besides, I intend to marry his widow."

Slocum gritted his teeth. *Over my dead body.*

15

"What we going to do now?" Jones asked.

Slocum studied the gray shack from their vantage point above the small outfit. Ever since he had heard Yarborough's brag about getting rid of Jim and him going to marry Ruby, he'd been upset.

"Let's go back to Fort McDowell. Those cattle won't be here for two more days."

"You think the cattle're stolen?"

"Why change brands after you get them if they aren't stolen?"

Jones nodded.

"When we get back, I'm sending you after a deputy I know in Mesa. His name is Dulvain. Tell him about the stolen cattle, then when he understands what I'm planning, you go by the store and tell Yarborough that Hanky sent you and he must come up there at once."

Jones bobbed his head. "You think it will work?"

"Be a good try."

"What are you going to do?"

"Keep my head down."

"Maybe get some sleep?"

"Yeah, I could sure use some."

"Come, you can sleep at my place. My woman will keep an eye out and feed you. You will be safe there. I should ride now to Mesa?"

"In the morning'd be soon enough."

After a full night's rest, Slocum awoke and ate some flour tortillas and frijoles Madonna cooked for him. The girl, hardly out of her teens, was Jones's wife number who-knew-what-number. On the thick-set side, she swirled around in her many pleated skirt and low-cut blouse. Jones had left for Mesa before the sun was up, to beat the desert heat.

Slocum sat cross-legged and nodded in approval at her cooking. She poured him coffee in a rusty tin can that gave it a different flavor, but he was grateful after the long absence during his stay with the Mormons. The rust made it taste better.

"Good," he said, not knowing her English capabilities. "*Muy bueno*."

She began babbling in Spanish at him.

"You and my husband were Army scouts together?"

"Yes, with Crook."

"They call him Gray Wolf?"

"Nan Tan Lupan. Yes, him." Satisfied, she smiled at him and nodded. "More tortillas?"

"No, this is enough."

He excused himself, promising to come back that evening for supper. On his bay, he crossed the Verde, where several bare-breasted Indian women were washing clothes. They giggled, elbowed each other and waved at him in passing. The skirts they wore were soaked as they knelt on their knees in the stream beating the dirt out of their wash. Their various, large and small brown breasts waved in the early morning's golden glow. He rode northwest.

His purpose for the day was not the bare-chested maidens, but rather Riley's movements in that direction with the stolen cattle. From the high places he searched for any visible dust in the north. Cattle in any numbers boiled up lots of dust. Heading north along a hogback, he saw some veils or wisps of what looked like dirt closer to the mountains and farther up the Verde. When they would arrive at Yarborough's depended on how hard the rustlers pushed them.

It was all going to be a big gamble. When the herd arrived, if Jones could convince Deputy Dulvain to come, and also if he could convince Yarborough to join his foreman . . . But it would be well worth waiting for if he could pull it off.

Midday, he got close enough to see the lead steer coming through the mesquite in his telescope. If Riley was driving them hard, they'd be to Yarborough's ranch in another day. Laying on his belly and collapsing the brass telescope, Slocum shook his head. It might not work. Not enough time for it all. Nothing he could do but wait. He slipped carefully back off the high point and climbed down the cholla-infested mountainside to his horse in the dry wash. Then he mounted up and headed back for Fort McDowell and the wait.

Madonna made him supper, and when he finished, he thanked her in Spanish. Then he smoked half of a dry cigar from his saddlebags, one that he had forgotten about. The luxury of the smoke filled his lungs and relaxed him. She came over and sat on the ground close beside him. With a tin plate covered in steaming beans and several tortillas, she began to feed herself.

"You have wife?" she asked in Spanish.

He shook his head.

"You need one?"

He shook his head again.

"She would cook for you and wash your clothes."

"You have someone in mind?"

She snickered. "Some of those girls at the river this morning said for me to ask you."

"No, I don't need a wife."

She bobbed her head as if satisfied and went to feeding her face, scooping up beans on the tortilla.

"Tell them I am flattered."

"I think they would be too," she said, and a devilish look of mischief glinted in her eyes. "They would be better than using your hand." She made the sign of jacking off with her right hand.

"Oh, yes."

"Good. You get horny, you tell me. I get one for you."

"I will, I will," he promised. All he needed was a big fat squaw in his blankets. He closed his eyes to the notion. Perhaps if he drank enough *tiswain,* the sweet beer these people made from fermented corn, or just plain whiskey, he'd try one of her friends. He drew deep on the cigar; for now though the idea had no appeal.

She went off to her wickiup, and Slocum to his blankets behind. Dogs barking woke him up. Soon Jones squatted beside him. "That Deputy Dulvain and two more are coming. They not ride through Lehi, come across the Salt."

"Good, the cattle are coming. They will be there tomm—today I guess. What about Yarborough?"

"I gave him message." Jones smiled. "He told me tell Hanky, he would be up here at noon."

"When do we meet those deputies?"

"Middle of morning across the river. They didn't want anyone to warn the rustlers that they were up here."

"Good idea."

"Oh, this Deputy Dulvain?"

"Yes?"

"He says Riley is big-time rustler and he wants him bad too."

"What did he say about Yarborough?"

Jones nodded. "He hopes he can make it stick on him too."

"So do I." Slocum glanced at the stars. He better get up; they had a big day planned.

Midday, they met Dulvain and he introduced two more men. Guard Tankersley, a range detective for the Arizona Cattlemen, and Maricopa deputy, Baisel Threadway. Both men looked to be in their thirties, dressed in suits, in contrast to Dulvain's cowboy gear.

"We actually need Yarborough there, when we ride in," Dulvain said, and others agreed. "We knew there had to be a tie to rustling and the Army beef sales. Got close to it twice. Last beef allotment, some Texan delivered it to Fort McDowell. Yarborough and his forces couldn't get any stolen ones, I guess.

"I met the man drove them in. Nelson was his name. He gathered those in Mexico. I checked it out. He wasn't in it with Yarborough," Dulvain said. "Tankersley thought we'd catch Yarborough that time, but he must have been warned. That's how come Nelson got the contract."

"I wondered how Nelson got it," Slocum said.

"Legitimate enough. If we can catch Yarborough in the camp with the rustled cattle, him and his bunch can break rocks in Yuma for a while," Tankersley said and nodded as if that suited him.

Riding slowly north along the same route that Slocum used the day before, they eventually saw the cattle's dust rising over the cottonwoods along the river. As they rested their horses on the hill, a plan was devised. Tankersley, Slocum and Jones would go around to cut off any escape to the north. The two deputies would be sure to sweep in behind Yarborough and then close the net on them.

All in agreement, they rode their separate ways. Jones led his group across the tough country studded with saguaros, ocotillo and barrel cactus. Large patches of pear had to be circled, and the clusters of cholla avoided, for a spiny pad in the fetlock region of a horse could cripple it. They moved through the deep ravines to keep their dust down. In two hours they were at the Verde, and crossed the knee-deep water on their mounts, to find that the herd had passed that point earlier.

Jones and Tankersley went up a mountain trail to cut off any escape to the north. Slocum rode up the cattle tracks to cover any attempt to escape in that direction. When he reached the side road, he saw that it had been churned up by hooves. He also saw where the thin tracks of Yarborough's buggy had gone ahead. His heart rate quickened. If Dulvain and Threadway were in place, they might get the whole bunch.

He came around a large paloverde tree and saw the two deputies with their guns drawn. A handful of dusty punchers stood with their hands high. A puff of smoke from the doorway of the shack and Threadway went down.

Slocum drew his pistol and drove the bay forward. His gun answered the one in the shack, and Hanky came stumbling out holding his guts. The Colt still in the man's hand, Dulvain cut him down, then whirled back to face the four rustlers.

Off his horse, Slocum helped the wounded Threadway sit up. "How are you?"

"Damn scratch," the man said, looking at the bloody sleeve of his coat. "Yarborough's getting away."

"He won't go far," Slocum said as he saw Jones headed uphill on his hammer-headed gray, the rifle ready and him pressing hard after the escaping man.

"He's going to get away," Threadway protested.

"Not from the best damn scout in Crook's command, he ain't."

"You mean Jones?" The man relaxed and Slocum took off his coat.

The wound was a deep cut across his upper arm. They

removed the bloody shirt and soon made strips from the garmet to wrap it with.

"Well, Riley," Tankersley said, swinging down from his horse. "This time we do have the goods."

"I bought them cattle," the sharp-featured rustler said. "I bet—"

"Get over here," Dulvain said. "Hanky's dying."

Slocum came over, satisfied that the deputy's wound was repaired enough for the moment.

"You shoot them two burglars?" Slocum asked.

"Yeah," Hanky admitted. Pale-faced, he laid on a blanket. The blood seeped out of his wounds.

"You kill Jim Branch?"

"Yeah—" Hanky coughed. "He was on to Yarborough's short weights."

"Yarborough order it?"

"That man's a liar!" Hands high, the businessman came down the hill ahead of Jones and his gray horse, at the point of his rifle.

Slocum leaped to his feet, blind with rage, and drove his fist into Yarborough's gut. The force of his blow made the man give a great exhale, then a roundhouse fist raised him off the ground. Yarborough flew backwards onto the ground.

Finished, Slocum turned to Dulvain, rubbing his sore hand.

"He's dead," the deputy said, motioning to Hanky.

"What did Hanky say?" Slocum demanded to hear the confession again.

"That Yarborough hired him to kill Jim Branch."

"Lies! All lies!"

"Except it was the statement of a dying man," Tankersley said and handcuffed him.

"When my lawyers finish with you—"

"You'll be damn lucky not to be wearing a necktie," Dulvain said to silence the red-faced Yarborough.

Slocum went and found his bay horse. He led him back.

"I owe Jones for five days at two dollars a day. Can Maricopa County afford to pay him?"

Dulvain nodded. "What do we owe you?"

"Nothing. Justice will be served."

"Exactly. You leaving?"

"Want the Arizona Cattlemen to pay Jones your reward too?" Tankersley asked.

"Yeah," Slocum said. "That squaw of his needs a new dress or two."

"How much?' Jones asked.

"A hundred dollars."

"Good. You ride through Fort McDowell again," Jones yelled after him. Slocum simply waved when he heard the ex-scout and trotted the bay southward.

Long after dark, he rode up Ruby's driveway. The pups barked, and she soon came out hushing them and wrapping a duster around herself.

He dropped heavily from the saddle and she hugged him, burying her face in his shirtfront. He slowly broke all the news to her—about Yarborough, and Hanky murdering Jim, and the rest.

"Oh, Slocum, how can I ever repay you?"

He held her tight. He owed her for all she'd given to his former partner Jim. A home, children—all of it. Damn, Jim sure didn't deserve to die in a raging river at the hands of a killer. Slocum rested his chin on the crown of her head. Only thing he knew—he couldn't stay there; word would be out soon enough.

The next night he stopped at the Gila and made camp. He wanted to go by and check on Cyra, Ramsey and Brown before he rode out of the territory. Had Nelson dropped in to see them? No telling, he decided, seated on the ground, pulling on a roll-your-own smoke and observing the red glow.

Two days later he made it to the Three Bar C. Coming

across the flats from the north, he saw her sweep away the hair from her face at the edge of the ramada. Then she drew up a rifle and looked hard at him.

"Cyra!" he shouted.

She waved and put the rifle back. He rode on into the ranch.

"Slocum, I didn't expect you."

He dismounted and dropped the reins. She ran over and hugged him. "We've had hell since you left."

"Why?"

"Those two bounty hunters been back twice."

"What did they do?"

"Got rough."

"Hurt you?"

She shook her head.

"They still in the country?"

"Ramsey saw them near the bachelors' camp a few days ago. They captured six men there and took them to Lordsburg for the rewards. You need to ride on as quick as you can."

He shook his head. Radamacher and Delaware had been responsible for Rosa's death. He needed to settle with them once and for all, before he left the country.

"A man named Nelson drop by?"

"No, why?"

"He's a man looking for some roots, thought he might drop in."

"How have you been?"

"Fine, I've been farming. Gathering corn and alfalfa hay."

"Can you stay long?"

"No. But I need to settle with them two bounty hunters."

She looked at him with fear-filled eyes. "They'll kill you."

"No," he said. "They missed their chance the first time."

"Can you stay for a short while?"

He looked off at Mount Graham. The great reddish purple mound reached into the azure sky. "Not long."

"Then hurry," she said and began to undo his gun belt. She let it drop and undid his pants. "We don't have much time then."

He shook his head. "Oh, we can take time for that."

"Good," she said and began undoing the buttons on her dress.

16

Long after dark, Slocum dismounted his horse before the house they said belonged to Ripple. He hitched the horse to the rack, looked around the dark street and went up to knock on the door of the adobe dwelling.

"Yes?"

"Slocum, sir. I need a word with you."

"Slocum—get in here. Why take such a risk?"

Herded inside the man's house, he nodded to a pale-faced young woman with a cup and saucer in her hand.

"My wife, Darlene. This is the man I told you about—Slocum."

"Yes," she said, but Slocum could tell he made no impression on her except he was a dusty ruffian who had entered her neat, clean house.

"Come out on the patio," Ripple said and showed him the way.

They took seats on wooden benches and faced each other.

"Now, what can I do for you?"

"Those two bounty hunters Delaware and Radamacher still in the country?"

"Yes, two weeks ago, they took six men off the track crew and only one was a valid arrest."

154

"They don't have many principles."

"I agree. The sheriff and I had a shouting match. I accused him of encouraging those two."

"Where are they now?"

"I understand they rode to Tombstone."

"I'll go look for them over there."

"How can I help?"

"No way, you've helped enough. They have been bothering some of my friends over in Arizona ever since I left here."

"You ever need anything—send me word."

"I will."

"Ramsey has made a heckuva good supervisor. Thanks."

Slocum smiled and nodded to the man. It was time to shake the dust of Lordsburg from his person. He would need a disguise to go into Tombstone. Maybe simply clean up and go in as a miner—lace-up boots, onetime washed Levi's two sizes two big, galluses and a canvas shirt. He'd need one of those cheap four-crowned felt hats with a wide, stiff brim. Clean-shaven, they'd never recognize him.

So he stopped off in the small town of Steins and bought his entire new outfit for a total sum of twelve dollars at a small dry goods store. Not changing into his new garments, he rode on west. He made his next stop in Sulphur Springs Valley, where he found a barber and bathhouse at Pierce. After his hair was cut short as a preacher's son and he'd been shaved clean, he took a hot bath in a copper tub in the back of the shop. Then in his new duds he went across the street to the cafe and had a supper of mulligan stew.

Feeling the role of the freshly arrived miner, all he lacked was a pick on his shoulder. He boarded his horse and saddle with a Mexican family until he could return for it, and caught a ride on a freight wagon to Tombstone. When they came out of Gleason, he could see all the bustling activity on the mesa—the around-the-clock shifts of men working deep in the bowels of the earth, hard-rock mining out the richest silver ore. A giant wagon freighted the ore down to the crusher you could hear even ten miles north. It shook the very earth and the smoke from the smelters stained the sky.

Wagon and cart loads of firewood were on the road, the fuel to fire the great furnaces that melted out the silver into bullion. Men denuded the mountains for this precious commodity. They passed small burro trains that brought the sticks for home fires and cooking. All were going to fuel the great needs of the silver empire.

Stretched across the mesa were over twelve thousand people, from whores to grand dukes, the largest city between St. Louis and San Francisco—queen of them all, Tombstone. Here there were more saloons than most places on earth, where the whiskey flowed freely and gambling went nonstop from dawn till dawn; where every kind of, shape or size of a dove known to man would turn you a trick for some pay. It was the ideal trap, where the miners making the outrageous wage of three dollars a shift could come up the shaft elevator and find any form of sin they wanted to waste their money.

This system would keep them going back down for their next shift and not saving their wages to go home on. It was purposeful, and the mine owners condoned it because they knew men that were well fed and bred stayed put.

Enter into this Sodom and see the naked woman in her trapeze on the stage at the Bird Cage Theater. Oh, sure she wore gauze in the painting, but her bare skin was what they saw, when seated at the tables or watching her swing while being jacked off in the small balcony rooms that overlooked the main floor.

Close the blinds and lay the girl down on the narrow cot. Why, twenty minutes from now she can have another hard-peckered one climbing on her for his share of her ass.

Slocum was familiar with all the sins of this place: the wheels of fortune in the saloons that plucked the suckers' money; stone-faced gamblers in the smoke-filled room underneath the Bird Cage stage, where poker went on twenty-four hours a day.

When he climbed off the freighter's high seat in the late afternoon and threw his head back to stare at the false-front signs on the corner of Allen Street, he knew he had arrived at the most sin-filled place on the western map of the United States. Some others would try to imitate it, but Tombstone in her prime was best of the worst things in mankind.

Slocum waved to the driver in gratitude for his transportation and started for the boardwalk. Somewhere in this crowded place that reminded him of the flesh-eating larvae of the screwworm in an animal's wound were two men he wanted to settle a score with—Delaware and Radamacher.

First he needed to find them. He started in the Bucket of Blood Saloon. He eased inside the noisy interior, where the crowd "bucking the tiger" were so vocal they hurt his ears.

"Check the gun?" the bartender asked.

Slocum frowned and then recalled the law about arms in Tombstone, undid his gun belt and handed it over.

"Ain't my law."

"I know. How much is beer?"

"Icy cold beer is a dime!" the bartender shouted to his question.

He nodded for one and, like a greenhorn there for the first time, looked down for the brass rail to set his right boot upon. That in place and his elbows on the bar, he watched the bartender return with a schooner of beer.

"Free lunch is over there!" the man shouted over the clamoring gamblers' voices.

Slocum nodded, knowing that for the ten cents he paid the man for his beer, he could fill his stomach with boiled eggs, oily sardines, pickles, hard rolls, butter and some sort of smoked meat. God only knew the source. He availed himself of the free food and soon decided the pair wasn't in this establishment.

So his quest went up and then back down Allen Street; it began and ended without success. No word was mentioned about Delaware and Radamacher, though he kept a sharp ear atuned. He found no trace of them. No sense giving away his hand, so he asked no questions as he mixed and mingled in the bar crowds.

Word could get out if he quizzed someone concerning the pair's whereabouts, and soon the two would be on their aware. His mission was to learn and not let them in on his plans. It would be slower his way, but also safer and surer. So he took a room in a cheap place for twenty cents and hoped the graybacks weren't too infested in the mattress.

His cap-and-ball Colt still checked at the first saloon he had entered, he carried the small round metal-enclosed claim check in his right pocket.

Day number two, he spotted Delaware stabling a horse at the OK Corral. His first great lead, in the cover of the crowd, he followed Delaware to the Alhambra Saloon. The bounty man disappeared inside the batwing doors and Slocum allowed him to get settled. He lounged in front of the ice-cream parlor sucking on a straw like a hick for ten minutes, then he discarded it and entered the busy bar.

Taking a place between two men at the bar, he ordered a ten-cent brew. He dared turn around, holding the mug in front of his face and looking for the familiar beaded, holster tie-downs that Delaware wore around both legs. He spotted him at a monte table, and Del had his back to Slocum, so he took some pains to study the man.

Obviously, Del was wagering and losing lots of money. The source of such funds intrigued Slocum as he considered where Radamacher was at. In disgust and some loud profanity Delaware drew a large bouncer to his side and told him in no uncertain terms what he thought of gambling in the place. The man waved him toward the door with his eyebrows wedged into a straight line. Considering that the bouncer weighed over two hundred pounds and stood well over six feet tall—Delaware went out the door.

Quickly, Slocum finished his beer and then left the Alhambra. A half block away, he could see Delaware's straw hat peak was headed for the OK Livery, no doubt to get his horse and guns. Signs all over advertised all firearms had to be checked upon reaching town by order of Marshal Virgil Earp.

On his pony in the street, Delaware lashed him and rode south at a hard trot. Perhaps the bounty hunter was headed for Fairbanks on the San Pedro or Fort Huachuca. No telling, Slocum decided; he would need to expand his search for the pair. He hitched a ride on a freight wagon and reached the stamping headquarters about sundown. He checked the horse racks and found no sign of the thin bay horse that Delaware had ridden out of Tombstone a few hours earlier.

There were some Mexican cantinas across the river, so he went over there to check on them. In the starlight, he found the bay in a pole corral and decided that Delaware had gone inside the small Mexican-run cat house. There was lots of women laughing and screaming inside, and occasionally someone would come stumbling out the lighted door drunk and spent. Some potbellied whore would finally call after him from the door in a sweet voice, "Come back, my stallion. Very soon."

The customer would usually turn and smile big at her words, then shuffle off.

No sign of Delaware. Crouched in the dark shadows,

Slocum began to suspect the man might live there or be staying all night, since he had unsaddled his horse. Other customers coming out of the place got on their animals at the hitch rack and rode away.

Standing up to stretch his frame, Slocum wondered where the second half of the pair was at. Then he walked across the plank bridge and took a blanket for five cents to sleep on the ground among several snoring drunks on a patio.

Dawn, he bought some tamales from a vendor woman selling out the door of her adobe jackal. Eating them as he walked, he wandered back across the bridge and down through the mesquites until he could see the hip-shot bay still in the pen unfed or watered. He walked back to Fairbanks and swept out a saloon for a quarter. He spent ten cents for a shave from a Mexican barber.

Mid-morning, the bay horse stood still unattended, and Slocum caught a freighter going to Huachuca and hitched a ride with him. He found the saloons in the fort town were empty even at noontime. Most of them depended on the soldiers stationed there, and they came after duty. He looked at the two liveries and one wagon yard, but saw no horse like the one Radamacher rode out of Lordsburg.

Had the two parted company? Then when Slocum started across the street, he spotted Radamacher like a big toad on the spring seat of a buckboard coming down the street. In time, he turned his face and reached the board-walk to look back at the man's retreat.

Damn. Radamacher was headed for Fairbanks, no doubt to collect his partner with the conveyance. Slocum half ran as he cut through between some buildings. His ambition was to learn the bounty man's destination. At last, out of breath, he stood on a high point and watched the dust boil from the rig headed for Fairbanks.

Damn.

17

When he returned to Fairbanks via another ride caught with a man hauling the mail to Tombstone, he discovered the bay had been fed some sorry hay and watered. No buckboard in sight. No doubt the two bounty men were gone in it.

A short whore came out and gave the horse some sugar. Slocum wandered over and admired him like he was a great stallion.

"Hey, this your *caballo*?" he asked.

She laughed. "No, he belongs to a friend. You like him?" she asked.

"Oh, I wish I had a horse."

"What would you do with him?"

"Go look for a silver mine of my own in them mountains."

"Ah, my baby, you sound lonesome." She came around so he could look in her low-cut blouse and see most of her fist-sized tits.

"Not bad. Can I rent him?"

"No, Delaware would beat my ass hard if I rented him. He is gone to capture some deserters."

"Deserters?"

"Yeah, him and his partner go down to Mexico and catch them black soldiers that run off. Army can't touch them over there. Him and his partner go over there, get them drunk and bring them back."

"I see," Slocum said. So at that he knew how they earned all that money to gamble so freely and why they stayed in the area.

"I could make you feel real good," she said, running her small hand ambitiously under the Levi's over his manhood.

He shook his head. "No money."

"Maybe I do it anyway," she threatened.

"I need to find some work," He gently pushed her away. "I get some and I'll come back. What's your name?"

"Seamah."

"Mine's John," he said and took off at a half run, looking back at her like he could hardly resist. So he needed his horse or transportation to find this place in Mexico where they went to arrest the deserters.

"Come back," she cried after him. "You're a mucho hombre. I show you a good time."

He shook his head and hurried on. No time for the *puta*; he had business to attend to. He must go back for his horse. First he would need to backtrack, get his pistol from the saloon, then try to find out where across the border those two captured the deserters.

In a short while, walking on the road, he hailed a ride back with an ore wagon. Upon his arrival in Tombstone, he retrieved his Colt from the bartender, then set out on the road for Gleason. His efforts to get a ride went unheeded. Hot and dusty from the road dust churned up by rigs spurning his efforts to stop them, he stopped in a bar to wash away some of it.

"Where you headed?" a man asked.

"The railroad," he lied, since his horse with the Mexican family was that direction.

The man beside him was of moderate height with a small pot gut and a goatee. Slocum guessed him to be in his thirties.

"You had enough of this country?"

Slocum nodded quickly.

"Haven't found any rich claims?"

"No."

"Guess you'll go back east?"

"Yeah."

The man laughed aloud and shook his head. "Why do all you Easterners think it's so damn easy to get rich out here?"

Slocum looked at the man and shrugged. What was his purpose? To tree a stranger?

"My name's Ike Clanton."

"John Smith."

"Yeah, I met your daddy." Ike slapped his knees and caused a cloud of dust. "You get it?"

"Yeah."

Ike sobered and looked him over, then turned back to the bar and his bottle of whiskey and glass. "Damn fools."

Not anxious to proceed with the conversation, Slocum finished his beer and headed for the door.

"Good luck, Smith," Ike said, waving his glass after him.

Slocum nodded and went out in the bright hot sun. He set out in long strides, eventually catching a ride with a peddler to within a mile of the place where he had left his horse. The stiff Levi's had chaffed the insides of his legs, and when he came in sight of their jackal, he felt relieved.

He saddled the bay and paid the woman fifty cents. In the saddle at last, he headed south down the wide grassy valley marked with some farmsteads. In late afternoon, he approached a ranch. He realized it was a mistake when several armed men came out of the adobe house and eyed him suspiciously.

"What's your business here?" one asked.

"Riding south. Figured I might get staked to a meal."

"Not here!"

Slocum touched his hat and reined the bay to the side. Not like most ranching folks to turn down a man riding the grub line. When he knew he was beyond pistol-shot range, his back felt better as he trotted the bay south. At the base of a canyon filled with live oak, he approached a small jackal.

A Mexican woman with a ripe figure came to the doorway. Some dark-eyed children around her skirt, she nodded to his words in Spanish.

"What can I do for you?"

"I would buy some food."

"Get down," she said. "My name is Consulela. There is water for your horse in the creek. I will fix you some food."

He thanked her, gave her his name and dismounted. Loosening the cinch, he led the bay down the steep trail to the small stream. He and the horse took their fill of the cool water. Then he washed his face and hands, and dried them on the kerchief from his pocket. When he looked up, he saw the small brown faces peering at him. They fled at his discovery.

On top, Consuela waved him over to the ramada. He unsaddled the horse and let him loose with a trailing rope around his neck to catch him.

"Where do you go?"

Squatted on his boot heels, he considered her. With her bent over her cooking, he could see down her blouse at the long breasts. She wanted him to see them or she would have stood sideways to him. At last, he decided he could trust her.

"I'm looking for two men who catch deserters."

"The black ones?"

"No, they're white."

She smiled and shook her head to dismiss his reply. "These two are mean white men?"

"Yes."

"The ones they catch are black soldiers, no?"

"I guess. Do you know where they are?"

"Naco."

"That's on the border?"

"*Sí.* The runaways go over there and the Army can't bring them back. Those two bring them back across the border for the reward."

Slocum nodded. "You know them?"

She nodded quickly with a black mask of anger. "They have raped women in the canyon and robbed others."

"What did the law do about it?"

"We have no law here. They are in town. They are for white people. Who would care, huh? All Latino women are *putas*." She swept her thick wavy hair back. "So why would the law care if they are raped?"

He nodded that he understood the problem and shifted his weight to his other leg. "They killed a friend of mine."

"Ah, so you want revenge."

He agreed.

"They have a jacal near Naco."

"Can you show me how to get there?"

"I can have my nephew take you there." With a wooden spoon, she scooped out beans and tomatoes on a plate then put some corn tortillas on it for him. He sat down cross-legged.

"Would he go and see if they are there?"

She frowned and soon came to sit by him. She arranged her skirt demurely over her legs and shifted until she found a spot for her butt.

"These men know me," he said to explain. "I don't

want them to know that I am here until I can confront them. If I waited here until I knew they were there, it would be better."

"*Sí.* Tomas can do that." Then she acted in deep thought and at last spoke softly. "They might not use the jacal for several days."

"Would it be embarrassing for me to stay here?" he asked, looking around.

"No." Then she smiled as if exceedingly pleased. She reached for a jug wrapped in burlap and poured some red wine in a cup. First, she took a sip from it. Her dark eyes looked hard at him from over the rim, then she handed it to him.

"You have a husband?"

She shook her head. "He was killed by the Apaches."

"Sorry."

"He hadn't been drunk, he might have run away when they came to the wood camp."

Slocum nodded that he heard her.

"I'm not a *puta*."

"I never—"

"So you know. Now I must go find Tomas." She started to get up.

"Tell him I will pay him twenty-five cents."

"At that much money, he may never find them at home," she said and laughed. Then she spoke sharply for her three wards to get inside until she returned. They fled to the doorway and peered back at the stranger who sat under the squaw shade.

In a half hour, she returned, and with her came a youth in his mid-teens riding a burro. She wore a broad smile and acted very confident as she introduced him to Slocum.

"You may have to ride over there many times to see if they are both there," Slocum explained. "Act as if you have no interest in them. I must know when both of them are there."

"*Sí,*" the youth said.

"I told him about the pay," she said.

"Yes, and avoid them, Tomas. They're mean men."

"I will let you know when they both are there, señor."
He rode off to the southwest, using a stick to make the
burro trot.

"He's a good boy. Take off your boots and go out back
and lie in my hammock. You need a siesta."

Not about to argue with her, he went behind her jackal.
There he toed off his boots and slipped into the swinging
arrangement. He studied the leaves of the live oak over
his head. They effectively cut out the hard sun, and the
breeze coming out of the canyon made it comfortable.

Soon he napped under his hat. The arrival of some men
out in front awoke him. He felt for the butt of his Colt.
They were obviously eating food she dished out to them.
The tone of one man's voice he recognized. It was from
the ranch where they had denied him food.

He raised up and sat on the edge of the swing. The men
soon mounted and left.

"Who were they?" he asked when he came around the
corner.

"Laughreys. They rustle cattle for old man Clanton."

"They sure aren't friendly to a stranger. I came by their
ranch looking for a meal and got run off."

"They thought you were the law in that outfit." She
shook her head, amused.

He stood up and stretched. "They stop often?"

"Yes, going and coming from the old man's place in
Mexico. They get tired of their own cooking. They will
bring me some beef when they come back in a few days."

"So," he said flexing his shoulders, "many outlaws ride
by here?"

"Some, but they are always nice to me and my children.
Not like the ones you seek."

Slocum studied the setting sun. Far off in the west,

purple, red and orange colors flared the horizon. He hoped his young lookout did not get in trouble scouting those two for him.

The youth soon rode up on his fuzzy steed. "They went to the fort with three prisoners. I saw them on the road with that buckboard making dust headed west."

"You did good. Tomorrow, you can go back and watch for them again."

"*Sí,* señor."

First, she fed him supper in the growing twilight, then her small children. After they ate, she put them to bed in the house. She returned with tobacco and corn husks, and took a place beside him on the hammock.

"I am nervous," she said and did not look up. "I am not certain this was such a good idea. Maybe if I smoke a cigarette I will be more at ease."

"Consuela, I can sleep on the ground."

"No—I mean, I am not a coward. Please let me smoke one cigarette?"

Her fingers trembled so the tobacco fell in her lap. He reached around her, took the corn husk and picked up the loose tobacco from her dress. Deftly he twisted it, then stuck it between her lips. He struck a match that flared and held it cupped in his hand to the end.

She coughed on the smoke, but soon took charge of it herself. *"Gracias."*

"So the rustlers ride by here."

She blew out a mouthful of smoke. "You aren't the law, are you?"

"No, I could care less who steals what."

"Good," she said, sounding relieved, and leaned against him. "I wanted this to be so perfect—you and me. Maybe I am foolish, no?"

"No." He hugged her shoulder and she rested her head on him.

"Tell me a story."

"I once rode by this canyon. There were no casas here then. I was riding a stout mountain horse and leading a half dozen pack mules, with supplies for the Apache scouts in Sonora."

"No, Consuela was not here then. I was a silly young girl in Casas Grandes, ready to marry Armando Valdez. He was braggart, but I was blind. Oh, he was so handsome and he was twenty-seven. Old enough, my mother promised me, to be a serious protector and provider, not like those lazy boys my own age who loitered around the plaza.

"My mother knew nothing. Armando was lazier than any of them. He had me do wash, so he could go to the cantina and drink. He brought me here and said he would get rich cutting wood. Ha! He slept on the pile more than he cut.

"He was sleeping when the Apaches came through. He was the only one they killed in the whole camp."

"So you can't go home and you barely make it here."

"I do all right." She bent over and ground out the cigarette.

Then she twisted and kissed him. Her full lips sought him and her arms tightened. He enjoyed her hungry mouth and the feel of her in his arms. Soon they became heady with their kisses, and his hand sought the pear-shaped breast underneath her blouse.

She gave a sigh. "Mother of God!"

He lifted the material and worked both of them gently. Soon her nipples turned hard as rocks and she leaned over and kissed him.

"Take me," she whispered. "I'm on fire."

They both stood and hastily undressed. In a flash of her brown flesh she was in the hammock on her back and his stone-white body pursued her on top. Her legs veed, and between them he directed the head of his near-hard shaft into her. She raised her butt up to accept him. He drove himself deeper and deeper in the tight slot.

She began to moan with pleasure, and then her entire body stiffened and a flush of hot fluids flooded out of her. With her hand, she wiped the fallen hair from her face and groaned.

"So sorry, but I could not hold it a moment longer."

He quickly kissed her and shoved his dick back in her. "We aren't through yet."

"Good," she said and clutched him.

The fire began to rebuild, and walls inside her contracted in pleasure, swollen by the excesses of their lovemaking. Then his skintight head began to ache, and he drove it harder and faster, until, in a great dive, he came in a powerful explosion. Consuela fainted.

"You all right?" he asked when she began to come to.

"I am so drunk, my lover, I may float from this hammock."

"It's a long ways down to that creek."

"Ah, *sí*."

"You still nervous?"

She shook her head. "I was married to that lazy Armando for four years. Not once did he do that much to me."

They both laughed. In a short while, they were asleep in each other's arms.

An owl awoke Slocum. He eased himself from the bed and looked at the tall horizon for the first light as he dressed. But the Muleshoe Mountains towering over them would hide the sun for a long time. He went to the creek and washed his face and hands by the starlight. Perhaps this would be the day those two would stop at their jackal and he could go there and face them down.

"You don't sleep?" she asked, coming down the trail with a sack towel.

"I slept good and long enough."

"I'm going to bathe. Is that all right?"

"Certainly."

"I am not so pretty to watch."

"Who said?" He squatted down on his boot heels.

"Oh, once I was very trim and now I am a mother."

"You are a very good woman, Consuela."

"You say that to be nice." She shed her blouse and skirt and soon waded into the shin-deep water. She cupped it on her skin, then she sat in the stream, washing and rinsing.

"A good man will come along one day who can stay." She looked over at him. "You have no roots?"

"No roots."

"I can understand. There are my three children."

"Not that. What happened long ago still haunts me."

"I see."

She rose and he toweled her off with the sacking. Soon she was dry and stood on her toes and kissed him. "I will never forget last night. Oh, my that was so wonderful."

Shortly after sunup, Tomas rode by her place on his burro. She gave him a flour tortilla wrapped around some beans. He thanked her and rode on to check the pair's shack.

Mid-morning, Slocum was idly lying in the hammock when he heard the click of the burro's return. On his feet, he quickly strapped on the holster.

"Señor, señor. A gringo has been shot and is dying." It was Tomas.

"Where?"

"Around the mountain. You think Apaches did it to him?"

"No," Slocum said, not entirely satisfied, as a goodly number of renegades still hid in the Madres. He didn't need everyone in the canyon in a panic about an Injun raid.

He caught the bay, slipped the bridle on his head and, without a saddle, leaped on his back. "Show me the way."

"Oh, be careful," Consuela cried after him.

"Keep your eyes open," he said to her.

"I will."

With that, he set the bay after the boy, who had his burro in a short lope. They rounded the mountain and headed south across the chaparral flat. Tomas reined up and Slocum did too. There in the sand wash lay the body of a man facedown.

As he came down the bank on his heels, Slocum could see the tracks in the dry wash bed where the wounded one had pulled himself a long ways. Slocum stopped and frowned; the man looked familiar. He knelt, picked the man up in his arms, turned him over and brushed some of the sparkling sand from his mustache.

"Nelson, can you hear me?" he asked.

"Barely," he mumbled.

Slocum could see the fresh blood on the vest and shirt. "I'm going to have to pack you to a woman's house. It may hurt."

"Go ahead."

"Who did this?"

"Couple Messikins tried to rob me last night."

"Where are the boys?"

"Down in Mexico, holding some steers and—" He made a pained face. "Waiting—for me."

"Those robbers get your money?"

"I ain't dead, am I?"

"Close to it."

Several times Slocum had to take rests. The weight of the man in his arms was close to his own, and he could see the way around the mountain where Tomas had disappeared on the burro and leading his horse. Soon he saw Conseula coming leading the bay with poles trailing. She'd made a travois.

In relief, Slocum dropped to his knees. "Don't worry. She's bringing a horse."

"Doubt that I can ride."

"No, you can ride this one. What in hell is your first name?"

"C. J. is all I ever used."

"C. J. Nelson, you are about to meet a great lady."

"Who—what?"

"You be still. This woman is just what you need."

"Is he alive?' she asked softly, peering over at him.

"Too mean to die," Slocum said and put him on the travois sling. "You hold his hand. I'll lead the horse."

"Why? I mean hold his hand?" she asked, looking confused.

"So he thinks he's in heaven and knows he ain't dead."

"But why?" she asked quickly.

"He knows he ain't going to heaven, so holding your hand he'll know he's still alive."

"Such a strange thing," she said and looked at the sky for help.

"Ain't too strange," Nelson said and took her hand as the poles began to scoot along.

"How long you been shot?" she asked.

"Last night sometime."

"What happened to you?"

"They tried to rob him. *Banditos,*" Slocum said over his shoulder. "Find out where his horse is at. The big ugly roan."

She spoke up. "He says at the stables in Naco on this side of the border."

"Good. Now where are Robles and Chico?"

"He says down on the San Bernadino River. Waiting for him." She gave a short cry and he halted the horse.

Slocum rushed back and found her on her knees. He reached in and felt for the man's pulse. It was still beating.

"The old devil fainted is all."

"Oh! Thank God," she sighed.

"Take some . . . of my money and get them boys up here," Nelson managed to whisper and Slocum agreed.

18

Slocum waited until dark to ride into Naco and claim Nelson's big roan. He left the bay at the stables. The roan was tough as iron wood and would be what he needed to ride to the San Bernardino. Conseula's neighbor lady, Juanita, had dug the bullet out of Nelson's upper chest and then cauterized the wound with gunpowder set afire. Nelson passed out, but he was breathing even enough and Juanita said he would live. So Slocum rode out to find the two boys and Nelson's herd.

He rode all night and only rested a few hours at the Slaughter ranch at the San Bernardino Springs. Slaughter, the rancher, an ex–Confederate soldier, wasn't there, away on business, but his brother-in-law and foreman showed Slocum to a small jackal where he could sleep a few hours. The man knew nothing of a herd in the south and the Slaughter holdings went far down the river.

Slocum slept until sundown and then set out in the twilight to find them. He stopped in a small village on the south end of the ranch. No one he spoke to knew about a herd. This country had been vastly devastated by the Chiricahua Apache raids moving down through there, coming and going to the Sierra Madras when they ran away from the San Carlos Agency.

The next day he spotted a rider on a familiar-looking horse, and the man looked hesitant about him keeping a parallel course to his. He finally decided to run him down and set the roan into a hard run. The man fled, but had no horse for the challenge.

"Wait! Wait!" Slocum shouted in Spanish. "I won't harm you."

At last the rider reined up and raised his hands in surrender.

"Where is Chico?" Slocum demanded.

"Where is the *patrón*?" the wide-eyed Robles asked.

"The *patrón* was shot, but he will be fine. Where is Chico?"

"Following the rustlers." The youth pointed to the hills to the east.

"How many of them?"

"Maybe six, they took the cattle and ran away. We could do nothing."

Slocum nodded looking in that direction. He saw no dust. Either they were far to the east or had stopped. Maybe with no more than teenage boys to chase them, the rustlers had no fear and were resting. He glanced down at the lathered roan who danced underneath him.

"Where are the other horses?"

"The rustlers have them."

"We better take up those tracks. It'll be dark before we can do much."

They trotted their mounts and headed northeast at Robles's direction. By twilight, Chico came in to join them.

Slocum explained about his *patrón* to the excited youth. It took some time to calm him down. The rustlers were less than a few hours' ride to the east. Weary and without food, Slocum said they should sleep a few hours then get in closer under the cover of darkness.

"What can we do?" Chico asked. "We have old pistols."

"Make them believe we are Apaches."

"But there are only three of us."

"Three Apaches can scare more Mexicans than ten guns."

"How?"

"We need to make some bows and arrows."

"In the dark?"

"Then some spears that we can hurl in their camp with flames on them about daylight." Slocum was not to be turned away. He intended to scare those rustlers out of the country.

He reached back and patted the two bottles of whiskey in his saddlebags—Nelson's liquor cabinet, which he'd noticed was there when he saddled the roan, choosing to use the man's good saddle on the animal rather than his old hull.

Finding sticks to use for lances in the dark proved harder than Slocum had estimated. But riding around in the starlight, they discovered an abandoned ranch headquarters, and soon the five- to-six-foot-long, straight sticks became no problem.

In no time, Slocum had the boys using a sling and hurling the sticks off in the night. They tore up a good shirt that Nelson also had in the pouches for the torch. Armed with their spears, they worked in the direction of the rustlers and the herd.

Slocum made them go on foot the last quarter mile. He carried the saddlebags and Nelson's rifle, and each boy was outfitted with an armful of "spears." They soon were close enough to the camp to smell the burning mesquite fire.

Slocum made his warriors sit down and wait. They acted fairly brave, but he knew they had never been under fire like this would be.

"When I give the signal to scream like Apaches, you never quit. Then hurl the flaming spears as fast as you can. I'll go to shooting."

He heard someone up pissing in the night. He nodded to the boys. Dropped on his knee, he could make out the silhouette of the pisser. He took aim and fired. The rifle shot crashed the still night. Chico ignited the dry grass pile with a match and they began screaming like banshees. In a moment, among all the confusion in the camp came the flaming spears like fireworks.

The terrorized screams of the rustlers filled the night. They ran like flushed quail, with only a pistol shot or two at the attackers. Knelt down, Slocum used Nelson's rifle to encourage their departure with sporadic shots. At last, in the dim light, there was no sign of any resistance. Filled with cautious relief, Slocum stood up.

"What now?" Robles asked.

"Gather the cattle and get all their horses, so they can't chase us."

"Whew!" Chico said and smiled. "This worked." Then he and Robles were gone for the horses.

When the first purple light began to spread over the plains, the longhorns and loose horses were in a trot headed for the San Bernardino. There was a boy on each side to head them, and Slocum, on the roan, took the drag and watched for any pursuit.

Midday, they were on Slaughter land and Slocum eased them up. They reached an outlying ranch headquarters, and the Mexican in charge greeted them.

Slocum asked if he could hire a few herders so he and his men could get some sleep. The man agreed, asking questions about the rustlers that Slocum could not answer.

"We ran them off with flaming arrows before dawn. I never saw them."

"You and those two boys?" the foremen asked in disbelief.

"If you woke up to flaming spears stuck in your bedroll, what would you think?"

"Santa Maria, I would piss in my pants."

"That's what the rustlers did. You hear someone talking about an Apache attack, you will know they're rustlers."

"Yes, that is a good thing. The *patrón* would laugh about that."

"He's gone," Slocum said. "On business."

"The *patrón* will have a good laugh about it when he gets back." The man shook his head in wonderment

"Go get some food and some sleep," the man said generously. "My men will keep the herd together. I will take care of your horses and have them ready when you awaken. Would you sell me this great roan horse?"

Slocum shook his head. "Blue is not for sale."

"Ah, he is beautiful."

Slocum hurried for the ramada, where a woman waved to him. No sleep in two days had him weary. He might be too tired to eat. Light-headed, he walked swiftly for the shade. But her good food gummed in his mouth and even the red wine did not help. At last, he sipped some water and forgot about eating; then, waterlogged, he staggered off to sleep in a hammock.

When Slocum awoke, he learned that the boys had passed out at the table and had to be carried to their hammocks. Sitting at the empty table with a headache, he found the woman's food tasty and drank several cups of coffee.

In two hours, the herd was on the move and passed through the main ranch, and that evening it reached the eastern base of the Muleshoes. Concerned about the rustlers in the area, he warned the boys and barely slept himself, with the rifle and pistol ready when he wasn't on guard.

Dawn, they drove the longhorns around the mountain and he went to see about Nelson. Looking no worse for wear, Nelson stood up and smiled at the sight of Slocum on the roan. Consuela kept close to the man's side, looking concerned and motherly.

"The boys?" Nelson asked.

"Fine. The cattle are on the flats."

"How can I ever repay you?"

Slocum dropped out of the saddle and shook his head. "Not necessary."

"Come," Consuela said. "I have some food and will make coffee. You two can talk while you eat."

"A good woman," Nelson said and motioned his head toward her.

"Consuela is an angel." He winkled privately at her.

"You have any plans for her?" Nelson asked.

"No." Slocum looked off at the top of the canyon. He never had any plans that meant permanent. He dropped to his haunches under the shade. Nelson sat on a small stool, showing some discomfort, but still he was in good spirits for a wounded man.

"I can sell them to a butcher in Tombstone, who has a contract with the Army over at the fort," Nelson said.

"Need me to ride up there and close the deal?"

"I'll be able—"

Consuela shook her head. "Slocum better ride up there and do that for you."

With a small grin of pride on his face over her words, Nelson nodded in surrender.

"Any word from Tomas?" Slocum asked.

"They stayed one night at the jacal," she said, pouring fresh ground coffee into the boiling water.

How would he ever face down two those two killers? He turned his attention back to Nelson, and they talked about the butcher in Tombstone.

"I can ride up there and see him today. Make the arrangements and then the boys and I can drive them up there easily."

Nelson looked over at him, then lowered his voice so she couldn't hear him. "I won't be an invalid forever."

Slocum agreed with a nod. "I will ride over to Naco and get my bay horse from the livery." Then he confided with Nelson on how he could have sold the roan to one of Slaughter's foremen.

"Why don't you take him as payment when you have to leave?"

Slocum shook his head. "Too good for me." Then he recalled the money that Nelson had given him in case he had problems, and he gave the leather pouch back.

"Only money I took out was to pay the livery bill," he said.

Nelson nodded and dug out some double eagles. He counted out ten and handed them to Slocum. "I wouldn't have these cattle or my boys, if it wasn't for you. No, you keep it. The cattle will make me lots more money than that."

Slocum slid it in his pants pocket and thanked him. After eating, he checked on the boys, telling them to take turns going for food and pointing out how to find her place. Then he rode to Tombstone to talk to the German butcher, Krause, about delivery of the steers.

He found the man wearing a bloody apron and busy sharpening knifes. The butcher nodded as Slocum explained that he represented Nelson.

"Yah, when can you bring them now?" he said in a heavy accent.

"I'll drive the herd up closer and bring them in in small bunches. Your pens won't hold over fifty at a time."

"Yah. Yah. How you get them? Old man Clanton, he can't find any."

"Nelson bought his," Slocum said and, amused, Krause nodded.

"You tell him I pay him a two-cent bonus."

"Good. That will pay for some of his inconvenience.

The boys will drive in fifty head this afternoon."

"I be ready."

Slocum left the slaughterhouse and mounted the roan at the hitch rail. Not much happening in Tombstone, he reined him around and trotted back toward his herd.

In late afternoon, he and Chico delivered the first lot. Krause looked impatient, but accepted them, and they began to individually weigh each one on his scale. When they finished, Slocum gave the receipts to Chico for Nelson. The cattle by his estimation could have weighed more, but the two-cent-a-pound bonus would even things out for Nelson.

He was saddling his horse when three men rode up. He recognized them as the Laughreys.

"Damn, drifter, you sure found them quick," the older one said and spit to the side.

Slocum decided they were merely talking and offered no threat at the moment.

"Couldn't get any food."

"Guess we had that coming. Tom Laughrey."

"Nice to meet you," Slocum said, not offering his name.

"Well, boys, looks like we got snookered by a drifter and a boy. Good luck. Next time we'll damn sure feed you."

With a nod, Slocum rode out with Chico, who soon crowded his horse close when they were out of their hearing.

"They are *muy* bad outlaws—were you not afraid?"

He shook his head at the boy—there were lots worse folks in the country than the Laughreys. Where were those two killers, Radamacher and Delaware?

When he arrived at the herd, Robles told him that Nelson had hired some men from the canyon to help them herd the cattle. Consuela and Nelson were coming with a wagon to feed the riders. Slocum nodded. Satisfied things were going smooth with the herd, he gave Robles the delivery schedule.

"Tell them I went to Naco to get the bay horse."

"Good. Good."

By taking a short cut, he missed meeting Nelson and her on the road. Before sundown, he found the boy, Tomas.

"No sign of the two?"

"They drove into Naco earlier."

"Good. Here is what I owe you. You're a good boy. Now ride home."

If he started a gunfight with those two on this side of the border, it would be sure to arouse lots of problems. Bitter visions of poor Rosa's brutal murder niggled him all the way into town. He stopped at the livery and claimed the bay. The gelding on a lead, he rode on into the small village.

Hitching him and the roan at a rack, he began to circulate through the small cantinas. No sign of the pair. He looked across the open space toward the cantinas across the border. Except for a small shack that housed a sleepy-looking guard, people went back and forth across the border unchallenged. The U.S. Customs Office had a light on, but they were only concerned with goods, not people entering the country.

Slocum sauntered across there and pushed in the first cantina. They were all busy watching some bare-assed can-can girls who were kicking at them, giving all the leering men good shots at their butts when their skirts went up.

Much cheering and clapping came from their fans, and the piano player did his best on the tiny piano to keep the music up for their frolicking. No one in the place looked like the two bounty hunters. Slocum slipped out into the darkness. The place was too poor to have a boardwalk, and he was forced to step around drunks seated on the dirt with their backs to the walls.

"Money?" someone begged.

He ignored them and went inside the next cantina. There he spotted the familiar straw hat at the monte table. Where was Radamacher? Carefully, he slid inside, in the shadows along the wall. But his actions telegraphed *trouble* to the customers. A rush for the door by several made Delaware whirl around. His hand went for his gun, but the overhead lights blinded him.

Slocum's first shot struck him in the forehead, and he fell backwards on the gambling table. Under his weight, the table collapsed in the thick gun smoke that engulfed the room. Screams of the *putas* and the fear-ridden others trying to escape filled the air as they rushed out the front and back doors.

With a round table turned over and used for a shield, rolling it like a wheel in front of him, Slocum tried to see through the eye-scorching fog for the other bounty man.

Then two quick shots from the rear of the cantina cut through the night. Slocum did not answer them, but he ducked. He heard the clink of spurs and knew that Radamacher was retreating out the back. Running out front, Slocum ducked between the buildings. When he reached the rear, he heard someone scream in the night's darkness. Then silence.

He tried to see beyond the pens and saw nothing. Then a figure appeared with his hands up and waving a white kerchief as he came around the pen.

"Don't shoot. Don't shoot."

"Where's Radamacher?"

"He ain't going to be doing no more deserter business," the black man said.

"What happened to him?" Slocum, still suspicious, held his pistol on the man dressed in half an Army uniform.

"He run into a knife."

"Knife?"

"Yes, sah. He done took the last black brother he's ever going to back to the guard house." The black man used the side of his hand on his throat to demonstrate.

"Thank you," Slocum said and holstered the Colt. "I need to get back."

"That Delaware, he ain't going to either, is he, sah?"

"No." Those two weren't going to murder any more good women either. *Rosa, I did my part.* He headed back, crossing the open space that marked the border until at last he was inside the United States and drew a deep breath of freedom.

He could see the Mexican soldiers and an officer across the border at the saloon. Soon two men brought out Delaware's body and laid it in the dirt. A porch conference was held, then others brought up Radamacher's corpse and put it beside his partner's.

Slocum untied the roan, swung aboard and took the lead rope on the bay. By midnight, he rode up Allen Street in Tombstone, thinking about having a large meal at Nellie Cashman's restaurant. Then, in the crowded racks before the Alhambra Saloon, he spotted the familiar Appaloosa's spotted butt. Only one horse he knew looked like that and it belonged to a Fort Scott, Kansas, deputy, Fred Abbott.

He pulled down the brim of his hat and rode on. With a quick glance over at the bay horse beside his leg, he decided to take him back to Cyra and the others.

Dawn was coming over the horizon when he rode the roan up the dry wash. Coming up the steep grade, he saw her face change to a smile.

"I about didn't know you," she said and rushed over with her skirt in hand to meet him.

He dismounted heavily and found his sea legs. She curled her lower lip under her teeth, acting hesitant.

"I come at a bad time?" He looked around for something wrong.

"No." She shook her head. "They've gone to work already. Only . . ."

"Only what?"

"Coffee and I are getting married."

"Congratulations."

"I never thought I'd see you again—"

"Hey," he said, looking around to be certain they were alone.

"They're gone to working on the railroad. No one's here but us."

"Good," he said and gathered her in his arms. "You'll be happy. I couldn't stay around anyway." He looked over her head at the Dos Cabezos Mountains, holding her close to him. "I can drop by and visit again; can't I?"

"Anytime. You look tired. Rest here today and wait for them. They'll sure want to see you."

He shook his head. "I can only sleep a few hours. I need to ride on."

"Not make it awkward for me, huh?"

He nodded, then hugged her tight and kissed her.

"Thanks," she said when he released her. "I have some food. You've not eaten in days. I know you."

"Good, I can always eat, or do whatever you want to do." He smiled when he saw her look to the sky for help.

Three days later, he was squatted in the shade of a mesquite. Dirty Shirt Jones explained that Yarborough and Hanky were in jail in Phoenix, and faced many charges. The rustler was going to testify against them.

"Even Brigham Young can't save them," Jones said and grinned.

"How is she?"

"Oh, Jim's widow. She's getting married."

"To some old man?" He frowned at his friend.

"No. This guy lived in Mesa. His wife died. He is her age." Jones shook his head. "I can't think of his name."

"Never mind. Where are those women I saw washing clothes at?"

"Upstream." He gave a head toss of his unblocked hat.

"I need mine washed," he said, looking over his dust-floured shirt and pants.

"You look like you could use a bath all right too." Jones began to chuckle. Then he shook his head, still amused. "Maybe I should go warn them."

"Naw, they'll find out soon enough."

"Yeah, they will. I am telling mine to stay at the wick-iup today." Then Jones laughed out loud.

The two shook hands.

"Sell me that roan?" Jones said as Slocum mounted the horse.

Reins held high, he shook his head. "Not for sale." Thinking about the giggling, brown-skinned maidens splashing in the water, he booted the gelding and headed for the Verde.

He twisted around and waved goodbye to his friend, drew a deep breath and made the roan trot.

Watch for

**SLOCUM AND THE
BOOMTOWN BORDELLO**

286th novel in the exciting SLOCUM series
from Jove

Coming in December!

JAKE LOGAN
TODAY'S HOTTEST ACTION WESTERN!